Season 70 Episode 1 - Eli

By

Kayla Renee

Season 70 Episode 1 Eli

Book one

Text copyright 2022 by Kayla Renee

Cover artist: bobooks

Published by Kayla Renee

Dystopian, fantasy, action.

"You can. You can do more than you think." -Eli

Friday, August 8, 2828

Eliot's girlfriend, Natalie, slipped her hand into his, sending sparks of pleasure down his body.

"Nat, is this spam?" He showed her the message that had just popped up on his phone.

Natalie's face paled as she looked at him. The two halted. Natalie pulled out her phone.

"But Eliot" - Natalie's eyes made contact with Eliot's - "we're in New Jersey - how?"

"Eliot Johnson!"

Eliot jumped, dropping Natalie's hand as he turned. Three men emerged from the crowd. Phones were being pulled out; screams and shouts filled the air as people were notified of the takeover. The three men, all dressed in a suit and tie and wearing dark sunglasses, stood in a V formation in front of Eliot and Natalie.

"We have orders for your removal."

"What do you mean by *orders*?" Natalie stepped in front of Eliot in a protective stance as her blond hair swept behind her in the wind.

Eliot tried to push her aside; he should be protecting her.

"Either come with us quietly or-"

Natalie socked the first man in the face. The man, distracted by the sudden gush of blood, took his eyes off the two for a split second.

"Come on!" Natalie practically ran Eliot over, grabbing his hand and pulling him down the sidewalk.

A man barreled into Eliot's side, ramming him into a brick building. Eliot struggled as his arms were forced behind him and tied. He heard a shriek.

"Natalie!" Eliot shouted.

"Get off me!" her voice commanded.

The man who had overcome Eliot pulled his arm hard, forcing him to stand up again. Eliot saw Natalie and two men forcing her under their control, her hands also tied behind her back.

People conversed in panic, dashing every which way, not noticing the couple's predicament. More men in suits emerged from different parts of the street corners, but Natilie and himself were the only ones being held by force.

Why? Why would they do this to us? Who are they? Eliot's mind tumbled. He turned his head just in time to see something black sailing for his face.

~

Ears rang. Muffled voices. He blinked his eyes open. He was in a large, circular room. Many, many people stared around blearily, looking like they did not know where they were.

"Natalie?" Eliot sat up so quickly his head spun.

She was laying on the floor, her hair spread out. In normal circumstances, this sight would have thrilled him. Her chest moved up and down as her eyes adjusted to the new area.

"You're okay!" He gripped her hand as she sat up, blinking hard.

A booming voice came over an intercom.

"Welcome, welcome! To the games! To go home, you must win the game!"

Eliot and Natalie looked at each other in confusion as a booming laugh sounded.

"Game? What game?" Natalie asked, looking around her.

Other people were stirring and muttering.

*"If you wish to live, you'll play, and if you don't, well…
You'll find out soon enough."*

Contents

Chapter 1 9

Chapter 2 19

Chapter 3 38

Chapter 4 61

Chapter 5 68

Chapter 6 83

Chapter 7 100

Chapter 8 109

Chapter 9 121

Chapter 10 131

Chapter 11 139

Chapter 12 147

Chapter 13 157

Chapter 14 176

Chapter 15 195

Chapter 16 208

Chapter 17 223

Chapter 1

Eli woke up with a start.

"Eli! Eli! We need to move! C'mon!"

Eli blinked his blurry eyes into focus. A tall girl with long, brown hair was hovering over him. Her coffee-colored eyes were wide with fright. He stirred, then realized that he was in the back of a car.

"They're coming, Eli! Wake up! We need to move!"

"Graw," he muttered, staring at her. She was pretty.

"Eli!" She shook his shoulder, striking him with the sudden fright that she must be feeling.

He sat bolt upright and immediately felt extraordinarily dizzy.

"Oof," he groaned, clutching his head.

The girl backed to the car door and flung it open. "Eli! C'mon! What is your problem?"

Eli blinked and shook the dizziness away. "What?"

"Eli!" she screamed so hard that her voice cracked. She grabbed both his legs and pulled as hard as she could, propelling him out of the car and onto the pavement. She was quick enough to protect his stunned head from smacking the ground.

"C'mon!" she insisted, pushing him.

He stumbled to his feet, and with her help, got a few feet away from the car. She stopped for a moment. He turned to stare at where they had come from, his mind full of a panic he could not decipher the meaning of.

A huge snow plow barreled towards the car, which was smashed up against a bent traffic light with its hood steaming. The snowplow rammed into the back of the car with such force that it crunched to the form of a smashed soda can. What was left could not have been more than a foot thick.

Eli gulped. "Um, what's going on?"

The girl looked at him. She had an interesting suit on. It was all white, as if she were going to be the backup dancer in a play or something.

"What do you mean?" she asked. She started backing up, forcing Eli back with her. Her eyes were still fixed on the truck, although she couldn't see the driver.

He stumbled along. "I have no idea where I am," he said.

"Good joke," she said, rolling her eyes. "You know, this is not the time."

"What joke? I - I don't understand."

"You idiot!" she raged.

Just then, a man got out of the truck.

She squeaked and pushed Eli into an alley out of sight. She pressed him against the wall with one hand and peered around the corner. Eli stared at her hair, which was swinging back and forth in a mesmerizing way.

"Who are you?" Eli asked.

She whipped back and glared at him. "You are so stupid! You know who I am and-"

She broke off and clapped her hand to his mouth. He struggled, but she punched his shoulder to get him to stop. He tried to say something, but she pressed her hand tighter against his mouth. He continued staring at her concerned face.

Footsteps echoed from a little way down the alley. They stopped. The steps turned and faded. She took her hand off his mouth and glared at him.

"This is *not* the time for a prank, Eli."

"Prank?" Eli was even more confused.

"Shh! We need to keep moving." She grabbed his hand, and he felt as if his stomach had just performed a somersault. She pulled him down the alley.

"No, really," he said as he stumbled along behind her. She was moving unbelievably fast. "Who are you?"

"Are you as stupid as I thought you were when I first met you?" she asked, looking back at him as she ran.

"Um… I don't know. We just met."

She stopped and rolled her eyes. "Fine, nitwit. Mia. I'm Mia. We have known each other for three years, and you are an annoying kid who is always ruining my day! Like you are right now! Happy?"

"Um, err, annoying?" Eli asked. "How? Three years?"

Mia, he thought, savoring the sound of her name in his head. Mia rolled her brown eyes and light seemed to glint off her brown eyes. Eli felt another flutter in his stomach.

"Yup. You are an idiot. I've been telling Addy that for ages. Now let's go before - get behind me!" She drew out two black handles that dangled from a silver chain.

Eli stared at her. "What?"

She grabbed his arm and pulled him so that he was a step or two behind her.

"Hey!" he protested, but then he turned around.

A man approached them. He had black hair, walked with a slight limp, and amber eyes. He glared at them and spoke in a gravelly voice. "You can't hide forever."

"We can try," Mia said, getting into a fighting stance with her arms ready for combat.

Eli looked back and forth from the man to Mia. "Hi. I'm Eli," he said, stepping in front of Mia.

"That's not what we do around here, idiot!" Mia screamed, fully exasperated.

The man stopped. "Thank you. That information will help us greatly."

"Now, see what you did! Get behind me!" Mia punched him in his back.

"Why?" he asked, turning to her.

Just then, the man grabbed him in a headlock and squeezed Eli's neck. Mia yelled in frustration and darted around the man. Other figures joined her, and suddenly, Eli was released, and the man was soaring up in the air as if he had been punched. Four other teenagers stood in front of Eli, all panting except for Mia.

A boy with black hair and a dark blue suit like Mia's was looking at her. "What went wrong?"

Mia rolled her eyes. "Nitwit here decided to forget his duty."

Eli snorted. All the teenagers looked at him.

"Excuse me, duty?" Eli asked.

A girl with yellow hair stifled a laugh. A girl in a purple suit and chocolate-colored skin nudged her warningly.

"Layla, Harper, stop that," Mia ordered.

"Sorry, boss," the girl with yellow hair said, flinging her hair back sassily. "We did not mean to interrupt."

"So, what's up with Eli?" the girl in the purple asked, stepping forward. Her dark hair was raised into a tight bun on the top of her head.

"Good question." Mia turned to Eli and approached him. He took a step back but had no problem with her getting close to him. Her eyes were mesmerizing. "Why are you acting like this? You know how important this mission was, and you fumbled it! *You told him your name!*"

All the teenagers gasped.

"You *what*, Eli?" the boy asked, appalled.

Eli looked at the boy. "Who are you? I don't know any of you."

The blond snorted again. "Good joke."

"No, really."

Mia glared at him so hard her eyes could have popped out of their sockets. "That's Layla the one in the yellow," she turned to the other girl, "that's Harper, and that's Bryce, and, in case you forgot, I'm Mia. Happy?"

"How could I forget your name? It fits you well," he blurted out. "Mia. So beautiful."

She punched him in the stomach. Mia stormed to the others as he spluttered and coughed. He straightened up and looked at the newcomers. Bryce was restraining himself from laughing, and Layla and Harper were staring at him in shock.

"What'd I say wrong?"

"Dude," Bryce said. "You are the bravest person I have ever met to say something like that to Mia's face. It's a miracle she didn't kill you."

"Shut up, Bryce," Mia snapped at him. Her fists were clenched as she paced back and forth. "We need to go back and report to Gideon. He will be most displeased."

"Oh, how fun," Layla said, rolling her blue eyes.

"And what's so bad about telling people who I am?" Eli asked, running his hand through his hair.

"Someone else explain," Mia ordered, looking like she was restraining herself from punching a hole in the brick wall behind her.

"Um, it's bad," Bryce said.

"Bad? That's a great way to say it!" Harper's voice dripped with sarcasm. "You could get killed for telling someone outside of your league your name."

"Um..." Eli felt a nervous shiver go up his back.

"Are you sure you are Eli?" Harper asked.

"Yeah, Eli was smart, actually smart," Layla put in.

Harper glared at Layla. "Shut your mouth!"

"*Quiet!*" Mia bellowed, actually punching the wall now, forming a dent a good three inches deep.

"Whoa." Eli stared at Mia. Brick crumbled to the ground.

"Let me think." She started pacing again and muttering to herself. The other three scuttled out of her way, pressing themselves against the stone wall. "Eli gets shot, the car crashes, he wakes up even more of an idiot than before. No bullet wound. Memory gone."

"Um, anything I can do to help?" he asked, eyes following Mia as she paced.

Harper gasped as Bryce grinned.

Mia approached him and leaned over him. "You can shut up!" She slapped him in the face.

"Wow. You are fierce," Eli said, his face stinging where her hand had made contact.

"Ugh!" She bolted off. She turned into a white streak and went out of sight.

"Um…" Eli said into the sudden quiet.

"Here we go again." Harper sighed.

"Fifth time today," Bryce added.

"And counting," Layla put in.

A streak of white appeared from the other end of the alley, and Mia appeared in front of the group again, barely panting.

"Let's just get you to Gideon, let him deal with you—oh, he is your brother, in case you forgot," Mia said.

Bryce stepped forward. "Um—" He cut himself off as Mia glared at him.

"What?"

"Shouldn't we finish explaining to him?" Bryce asked.

"No! I've had enough of his pretending. He will not dare pretend in front of Gideon." She gave Eli a nasty look.

"I have a brother?" Eli wondered.

"Quit the joking already. You've done enough today," Mia snapped.

"Mia, I think he's telling the truth. He really doesn't remember," Harper said, looking at Mia.

Mia spun on her. "Good for you. Let's just go."

"Where?" Eli asked, totally confused.

"No more questions!" Mia bellowed.

"That's rather harsh, Mia; the dude can't remember a thing," Bryce said.

"I don't care; he's ruined my day enough times already."

"Let's go then," Layla said and disappeared.

"Where did she go?" Eli asked, astonished and rather frightened.

Mia bit her lip to keep herself from snapping at him.

"Oh, you forgot how? You can come with me then." Bryce

said.

"Forgot how? What?" Eli asked as Bryce walked over to him.

"You'll remember soon enough, I hope," Bryce said as Harper disappeared when she closed her eyes.

Eli's mouth dropped open.

Bryce grabbed his wrist. "Close your eyes," Bryce ordered.

"Wait-"

"What?"

"What happened to-to the man who attacked us?"

Bryce shrugged. "I dunno. If he wasn't knocked out, he either teleported to his base if he was smart or somehow is still going up."

"Huh?"

"Eli, just close your eyes," Bryce insisted.

"Okay." Before closing his eyes, Eli's gaze fell on Mia, who was glaring at him. His heart fluttered.

Chapter 2

Eli opened his eyes.

"Wow." His voice echoed around and around a large, metal room lit with fluorescent lights.

Mia appeared in front of Eli and Bryce. She glared at him, then stormed away, the metal floor echoing her angry footsteps.

"So, how'd it go?" a regal voice asked from behind them.

Eli jumped so hard that he was surprised his skeleton didn't leap out of his body. Bryce nudged him, so he turned around. Up, on top of an elevated, metal platform, stood a buff young man. He was maybe twenty-one and had brown hair and stony gray eyes. He was staring hard at Eli.

"Um, do I know you?" Eli asked, bewildered.

Gideon's face changed. "Eli, any news to report?"

"Uhh…"

"Eli, stop playing games."

"Sir, um, Gideon," Bryce managed, stepping forward and motioning for Eli not to say a word.

Gideon's eyes moved to Bryce. "What?" he snapped.

Eli took a step back.

Bryce twisted his hands nervously. "Eli kinda lost his memory, and apparently, he can't remember a thing."

The man, Gideon, looked even harder, if that was possible, at Eli. "This is not the time for joking, young man. That could result in serious punishment."

Gideon's response was not very reassuring to Eli.

"No, really," Bryce put in.

"I can stand in for Eli."

Eli turned to see Mia coming out of the hallway. She unattached something from the back of her suit, and it disintegrated, leaving her wearing an oversized hoodie and baggy sweatpants. Eli stared. She slipped both hands into her pocket and came over to stand next to Bryce, not Eli.

"Mia." Gideon stared hard at her. "You don't believe this baloney, do you?"

"Unfortunately, I do." She glared at Eli. "Dufus here was shot, the car crashed, and when he woke up, he was even stupider than he had been before."

"I see." Gideon's calm response made Eli uneasy.

"Oh, and one more thing," Mia said. Bryce jerked as if he were restraining himself from covering her mouth. "He told them his name."

"What?" Gideon was up and on his feet. "What did you do, Eli?"

He stormed down the steps with fists clenched. Eli felt his blood start to leave his head. Who was this guy? Eli started backing up. That didn't help him, though, as Gideon continued approaching him until Eli was pressed against the metal wall, the coldness from the metal seeping through his clothes. Gideon's face was mere inches away from his face.

Eli gulped. "I... uh..."

"Gideon," Bryce's voice came.

"Quiet!" Gideon commanded. "Let my brother explain for himself."

Eli stared into those angry eyes.

"Um..."

"Eli, just tell him already." Mia's voice awoke his brain.

"I did tell them my name. I did not know why I should not."

Gideon bared his unusually pointy teeth. He leaned closer, and Eli had the nasty feeling that Gideon was about to bite him or something, but to his relief, Gideon whipped around and stormed towards his seat again. Eli remained where he was, pressed up against the wall, chest heaving.

"Eli? Is he back? Did I hear that you guys made it?"

Eli looked around at the unfamiliar voice. The strangest girl he had ever seen had walked into the room from a hallway. She had orange hair, the shade that did not seem to go with anything, and hot pink eyeshadow lined with green instead of black. On top of all that, she wore neon-yellow leggings, bright red lipstick, and a baggy red shirt. Her shoes were split-pea soup green.

"Addy." Mia sighed.

The girl's eyes were white, really white. She had the tiniest pupils that Eli had ever seen, and they were black. All black.

"Eli." The girl walked towards him. Her eyes were focused straight ahead, not really looking at Eli.

"Um, Addy," Bryce started to say, but with a look from Mia, stopped.

Addy walked right up to Eli and felt his face.

"Um…" Eli tried to lean away.

"It is you, Eli!" She stepped back and smiled a broad smile.

"Uh…" Eli looked uncomfortably towards Mia and Bryce.

"Addy can't see," Mia answered Eli's unasked question.

"She's blind," Bryce added.

"Why are you telling him that? He already knows that," Addy said, turning to Bryce and Mia.

"But-but…" Eli was at a loss for what to say. "How did you know where I was standing?" His mind could not comprehend the situation.

"It's her blessing." Bryce whispered to Eli.

"Huh?"

"We all have a blessing, you see-" Bryce started to explain, but Gideon interrupted.

"Just get Eli and everyone out of here. I need to think."

"Yes, Gideon," Bryce and Mia said in unison. Bryce grabbed Eli's arm and dragged him away.

"Addy, c'mon," Mia told the strange girl.

"Brother," said Gideon.

Eli stopped, remembering that Gideon was his brother. "Yes?" he asked uneasily.

"Get your mind straightened out. We will talk later," Gideon said, not even looking

at Eli.

"Um… Okay," Eli said, still totally confused.

"Let's go," Bryce whispered, tugging Eli down a metal corridor that led from the room.

~

"Where are we?" Eli asked as Bryce led him through a door and down some metal steps.

"Home base."

"Huh?"

"Home base. It's where we live."

"Umm…"

"How do I explain this?" Bryce asked himself out loud. They entered a brighter hallway with gold cylinders in its center to hold the ceiling up. "There is a battle going on, kinda. There are four leagues. We're League Four. This is our base. We are supposed to get the golden brick from League One. That's how we win."

"Umm… What happens if we don't get this gold brick?" Eli asked.

"The result is too terrifying to think about."

"What?"

"They'll kill us."

"They'll what?"

"Oh, Eli! You make this difficult - sorry, it's not your fault!" Bryce took a deep breath as if to calm himself. "Okay. So if you get the gold brick, then you get freedom and you will be able to live forever in the world for free, not totally sure what the *free* part means."

"Sounds great to me!"

"Yeah. Except for the fact that this has been going on for decades and none of the original people who started this game are still alive."

"Oh… Then how are we here?"

"The originals either died of old age or died trying to get the brick that could set us free, and well, naturally, they made families of their own."

"Who would want to play a game like that?"

"I guess a lot of people, and they did not have a choice. The government forced it on certain families."

"Then… Where are our - well, our parents?"

Bryce was quiet.

"Bryce?"

"They, as in yours, mine, pretty much everyone you know, parents… Have been killed…" Bryce looked away.

"Oh."

They turned down a hallway. Doorways lined each side.

"Um… So why does Mia hate me?" Eli asked.

Bryce's sad expression turned into a smug grin. "Oh. I love how you are so obvious with your emotions now! I didn't know you liked her before!"

"Who?"

"Mia."

"Um…"

Just then, a clattering of feet came from behind them. Eli jumped and pressed himself against the wall. When he looked back, though, Mia and Addy were hurrying down the metal hall towards them. Mia was still in her baggy hoodie.

"What's up?" Bryce asked, his face turning red.

"Just seeing what you guys are up to," Mia said, ignoring Eli.

"Oh, I was just going to show Eli our room."

"Oh." Mia seemed unusually relaxed now, as if all her anger had been drained when she took off her suit. "Um, Eli, you know you can take off your suit now."

The teens had all already shed their suits to reveal casual street clothes. Eli looked down, just now realizing his clothes were like Mia's, only green instead of that pearl white.

"I don't know how."

"Oh, like this." Bryce made a movement behind Eli as if he were unbuttoning a button at the back of Eli's neck. Immediately Eli felt more comfortable and looked down to see himself in a short-sleeve T-shirt with a large, strange-looking thing on it with sunglasses. It had the words *cool dude* written underneath.

"Better?" Bryce asked as the four once more started walking down the hall.

"Loads!" Eli said. He felt eyes on the back of his neck and

turned.

Mia was studying him hard. She looked away. "I just don't get it," she said.

"You don't get what?" Eli asked.

"You were the same person I knew up until you got shot. Now you're different."

"Is that a good thing?"

Mia studied him hard. "Maybe," she said. Eli felt another flutter in his stomach.

"So." Bryce broke the uncomfortable silence as Eli and Mia sized each other up. "Eli, want to see our room?"

"Wha-" Eli looked at Bryce. "Oh, yeah. Let's go." Eli turned away.

"Hey-" Mia caught his attention.

Eli turned to look at Mia.

"Um... I guess I'm glad you're not dead." Mia said.

"Thanks," Eli said, then turned back to walk with Bryce, whose shoulders were heaving with his effort not to burst out laughing.

"Oof!" Bryce grunted.

Mia had just shoved him from behind. "Knock it off," Mia hissed.

Eli could hear the two girls walking down another hallway, then the click of a door shutting.

"Man! You are the best new Eli I have ever seen!" Bryce chuckled.

"What?"

"It's obvious you're smitten with Mia! She hates the idea of any dude liking her!"

"How do you know that?"

Bryce turned bright red. "Here we are!" he said, looking away and opening a metal door.

Eli stared into the unfamiliar room.

"Your bed is on the left," Bryce said, going inside. The room had white walls, a white ceiling, and a white hardwood floor. There were two loft beds, both with dark blue sheets. Underneath each of them sat a desk and a swivel chair, a trash can, and a light. There was a closet on the left side. There weren't any windows.

Eli stepped in. "So...we bunk together?" he asked as the door swung shut behind him.

"Yup. It's cool. You're a good roommate."

"I am? I am. Okay..." Eli sat in the desk chair as Bryce hopped onto his bed. Eli felt like he had walked into a stranger's dorm room or something. He gazed at the desk in front of him. A bulletin board above the desk displayed pictures, all but one of which were from inside home base.

There was one of him, Bryce, and another boy, all smiling. There were more with him, Bryce, and some other people Eli didn't recognize. One of him with Gideon, and one with Eli, Gideon, a tall woman with brown hair, and a man with scruffy brown hair. Eli contemplated it, studying his own image. He seemed to be a decent-looking teenager with brown hair the same shade as his mom's hair and eyes the same shade as his dad's.

Then, his eyes slid to the last picture. Bryce, Layla, Harper, and Mia. His eyes rested on Mia's face for a long time. She was smiling, for once, but she stood next to Harper.

"I don't know how you're suddenly getting along with Mia, dude," Bryce interrupted.

Eli started. "What?"

"You two used to go toe to toe all the time. Always bickering and yelling at each other."

"Seriously?" Eli could not believe such a thing.

"Yup. It got pretty nasty sometimes. Like the time Mia got so mad she broke your arm."

"Um…" Eli scooted his chair back slightly.

"Don't be too worried about her. She's cool. You'll see."

"Okay…" Eli was at a loss of what to do. He got up and climbed up his ladder. Up top, he found a neatly made bed. The dark blue comforter fit snugly above his pillow. He pulled back the sheets and lay down with his hands under his head, staring at the ceiling.

"What's this blessing thing that Mia talked about earlier?" he asked. He looked over to Bryce's bed.

Bryce had been laying on his side, reading a book. "Huh? Oh." He set the book down and sat up. "We all have unusual strengths. No one is quite the same in each generation. We call them blessings. Addy, like you heard, can 'feel' what is around her even though she can't see. Mia, as you might have figured out, can run astonishingly fast."

"What about you?"

"I am exceedingly good at boxing," Bryce said, demonstrating in the air.

"So, you are the one-"

"Who made that guy sail into the air?" Bryce knew instantly what Eli was asking about. "Yeah. That was just a slight punch to the chin."

"Okay," Eli said. "What's mine?"

"You can fly."

"What?" Eli couldn't believe his ears. "You're joking."

"Am not."

"Prove it."

"You prove it yourself."

"But I don't know ho-"

Eli's protest was cut off abruptly, this time by a knock on the door. Bryce paled and gaped in horror at Eli.

"What's wrong?" Eli asked as he and Bryce climbed down their ladders.

"Um... Well..."

Eli opened the door. Right behind it was Addy, now dressed in a simple, peachy-colored dress. Her hair dangled from a ponytail.

"Ready?" she asked, eyes looking in Eli's direction.

"Um, for-"

"Excuse us a minute. We will be right back." Bryce shut the door in her face and put his hands to his head. "I'm an idiot!"

"What?"

"You have a date with Addy! I totally forgot to tell you because of you losing your memory!"

Eli stared at him. "I asked Addy out on a date?" Bewilderment filled him. If he were going to ask anyone on a date, it would be Mia. No question.

"No, she asked you on one, and you felt you couldn't refuse and said yes," Bryce told him rather desperately.

Addy knocked again.

"Umm…" Bryce looked anxous.

Bryce looked like he might pass out. He slipped out the door. Eli could hear talking, then Bryce slipped back in. "She didn't know that you forgot! Now, um - here, put this on!" He handed Eli a bowtie. "And here." He attacked Eli's hair with a brush, quickly smoothing it down.

"But-but-" Eli stuttered as Bryce forced the tie on him.

"You'll do great, man."

"But…"

"Have a good time." He shoved Eli out the door and shut it quickly behind him.

Eli stood stock still in the hall.

"So," Addy said. She looked quite good, despite her orange hair.

"Um… What now?" Eli asked stupidly. His hand fumbled for the door handle behind him. He moved to open it again and slip back inside, but Bryce seemed to be holding the door handle, refusing to let Eli back in.

"I thought we could go to Master Mind," Addy said.

"What's that?"

"It's a restaurant."

"Uh. Cool," Eli said, although he couldn't seem to remember what a restaurant was. "Let's go then."

The two walked down the metal hall, their feet making an echoing sound as they went. Something gave him a bad feeling about this, something in the back of his mind. He kept on fidgeting with his tie. Addy slipped her hand into his and looked up at him. She was at least a foot shorter than himself.

"So, what do you think of this place?" she asked.

"Um…" Eli scratched his neck. "It's um… strange?"

They walked on in silence. Eli took his hand back as they turned down another hall. Soon, they came upon a medium-sized nook where there were tables and couches.

Mia and Harper were sitting on a couch together, relaxing and talking. Eli looked at the two as they passed by. Mia's calculating look followed him.

"You really believe him, don't you?" he heard Mia ask when his back faced the two.

"Yes," Harper said confidently. "He could never act this long."

~

The restaurant lay beyond the base and down a few different streets. A bell announced their presence when Addy opened the door. Inside, the air was heavy with lurring aromas. A waitress regarded the two suspiciously, then led them to a table.

"Anything I can get you to drink?" she asked haughtily,

eyeing Eli with suspicion.

"Lemonade, please," Addy said.

The two looked at Eli.

"Uh...same."

The waitress left. They sat in awkward silence. Eli looked around. There were wide windows surrounding the room. The place was bustling with people.

"It's cozy in here, isn't it?" Addy commented.

"Uh, yeah..." He looked across to the row of booths next to them, and he spotted a familiar face.

The boy with chocolate-colored skin from the picture with him and Bryce. He sat in a booth with a girl whose skin color matched his. Two gruff-looking men were escorted to a table by another waitress as Eli looked on. The boy glanced up. His face broke into a grin as he noticed Eli and Addy. He spoke to the girl and came over to them.

"Hey, E!" he said.

"Um..." Eli looked up blankly at the person he did not know.

The boy's grin faded slightly. "El... E, what's up?"

"He lost his memory," Addy piped up. Eli continued to stare at the teenager in front of him.

"Oh, shoot." The boy's face blanched. "I'm T."

"T?" Eli asked.

The boy looked uneasily around, then bent close and whispered, "T is the letter of my first name; we can't give out our real names in public. You could die for that."

Eli's face flushed and sweat prickled on the back of his neck. "Okay…" he said, shifting uneasily.

"Hey, A. See you later." T hustled off to his booth.

Eli gazed after him in bewilderment, before turning to Addy. "Um, who-"

He stopped himself as Addy picked up a menu and stared at it aimlessly. Eli followed her lead. His eyes wandered the strange lines that squiggled along with the paper with pictures of food. Some were circles. Some had dots; some intercepted each other.

Their waitress came back with their drinks. "Ready to order?" she asked.

"Can I get the jumbo double cheese, please, with fries?" Addy asked.

Eli looked at the menu again. "Same," he said. The waitress wrote something down on a pad of paper and left without another word. More people came into the diner and were seated in spots near the two. Eli shifted. "So, um… What language are those menus in?" he asked after a long moment.

"English," Addy decided. "I think," she added as an

afterthought.

"Really? Because—aaaah!" Eli jumped out of his seat.

One of the waitresses who had been passing them had lost her balance. The tray of steaming soup spilled all over his and Addy's table, splattering Eli. The man who had been sitting behind Eli shot up and grabbed Eli while he was temporarily off his guard. Shocked cries filled the air as people noticed Eli's predicament.

The man forced him out of the booth as other gruff-looking men jumped up and made their way toward Eli. A dagger was put to his throat. Eli gasped and struggled. Aghast, people made a move to assist the boy, as if by some instinct that told them to help, no matter if he belonged to the enemy.

"Nobody moves or he dies!" the man bellowed.

Silence spread through the restaurant like a ripple in water. Eli's eyes were wide and frightened. Little gasps of air escaped Eli's mouth, but the blade cut his skin with the slightest movement. The waitress who had landed on the floor looked up at the man with wide eyes.

"Anyone with a lead on how to break down League One, come tell me, or Eli dies!"

Great, Eli thought. Now everyone knows my name.

No one moved. The man pressed the cold dagger even harder against Eli's throat. He gagged.

"No information? Pity." The man's hand tensed, ready to end Eli. Eli started to close his eyes when the girl with T stood up. T gaped at her, dumbfounded.

"No, stop!" she screamed. "I have a lead!"

Everyone turned their attention to her. Eli closed his eyes, just in case he was dreaming and would wake up to find everything that had happened had been in his imagination. Well, maybe everything but Mia.

Chapter 3

Eli opened his eyes.

"Good," the man who had a tough grip on Eli said.

The girl who was with T looked just as horrified as T did. The other men were still standing, their attention on the girl.

"Come with me," a gruff voice said. It was the man who had almost choked Eli just hours ago in the alley.

The girl started walking forward, but T grabbed her hand. "You can't go!"

"I have to," she said, looking at him.

"But, but-"

"It's okay," she said, setting her face determinedly. "Lives are in danger. I don't care who it is." She slipped her hand out of T's and started towards the man. Eli noticed the man's hand go to his belt, where a gun was holstered. T tried to stop them, but one of the other men grabbed him roughly.

"Don't go after them. Or it'll be worse for her."

The diner filled with an uncomfortable silence. The door

swung shut behind the girl and the man with the gun as they left the building. Eli struggled and found the dagger at his throat again.

Addy stood up, staring in Eli's direction.

"N-N-" he tried to tell Addy not to do anything. She could not see.

A few moments later, a loud gunshot echoed in the room, something thudded against the wall, then another gunshot sounded.

"No!" T shouted in agony. He tried to run out of the restaurant, but the man who had a hold on T jerked him back.

The man walked coolly back into the diner. S was nowhere in sight. "We're done here. C'mon, boys. We have a job to finish."

All the men but the one holding Eli started walking towards the door. The man's grip on Eli tightened as he readied the dagger to slit his neck when a bright red light filled the room and blinded everyone for a moment.

The man slackened his grip. Eli turned to see the man crumpled on the floor, dead. His head had been cut off, leaving a gaping wound on his neck. Eli's eyes went to where everyone else was staring. Addy. Her pupils glowed red and slowly faded to their usual black. She relaxed. The other men had not noticed a thing as they had already left.

"Ad - what?" Eli looked around.

T was staring at Addy in shock. "How?"

"We need to go - now," Addy said. She put some money on the table, grabbed Eli's hand, and dragged him out of the restaurant. T scrambled out of his booth and followed them.

As soon as they were out of the restaurant, Addy dragged Eli down an alley. There, crumpled in a corner, lay the girl T had been with. T rushed over to her. She had two bullet wounds, one in her chest, the other in her arm. She was unconscious.

"No! No! Silvia!" T sobbed, his body heaving with grief. He hugged her limp figure. "No, no, *no!*"

Eli looked on, unsure of what to do.

Addy rushed forward and felt the girl's pulse. She looked up, amazed. "She's okay," she told T.

"No, she's not!"

"Yes, she is! Feel!" She put T's hand on the girl's wrist.

He looked at Addy, stunned. "What? But, but-" He looked with horror at the girl's chest, splattered with blood.

"Who is she?" Addy asked.

"S-Silvia."

"I have never heard that name before," Addy said.

"She-she…" T trailed off.

"She's not in our league, is she?" Addy asked T. He sucked in a breath. "It's okay. You can tell me. We won't tell anyone."

"No." T's voice filled with grief. "And I promise with my whole heart, I did not know that she had a lead. I... I..." He stuttered to a stop.

Eli walked towards the two, studying the girl. The bullet wounds did not seem so bad now. Suddenly, the girl woke up with a gasp.

"Silvia!" T hugged her again. When he sat back to look at her, the girl backed up with frightened eyes.

"Who- who-"

"Silvia, I thought I lost you!"

"What? Where am I? Who are you?" She looked from T to Addy with wild eyes. Silvia's chest rose and fell with frightened breaths.

"Silvia, are you okay?" T asked.

"Who are you?" she repeated, pressing herself into the corner even harder.

"You know me!" T insisted.

"No, no, I don't." Silvia's eyes darted around her surroundings. "Where am I?"

The realization hit Eli as if he had been shot again.

"She can't remember anything!" Eli exclaimed.

Both Addy and T jumped and turned around, obviously having forgotten that Eli was there with them.

"What?" T asked.

"It's what happened to me!" Eli told them. "I woke up earlier today and couldn't remember a thing."

"Who are you?" Silvia asked again.

Tears sprang to T's eyes. "Silvia, I-I'm Travis. I'm your boyfriend."

"What?"

"You-you just got shot!"

She looked down at her chest, which seemed to have healed itself, like Eli's had. "I'm completely confused," she said. "Now, can I get out of here?"

"Silvia!" Travis tried not to shout.

"Shh!" Addy said. "Calm down. We need to get her somewhere safe."

"Who are you? Bring me somewhere safe? Why?" Silvia wondered.

"We can't bring her to base, though! She's in League Two!" Travis said in desperation.

"We don't have much of a choice right now," Addy pointed out.

"Gideon's gonna kill me!" Travis buried his face in his

hands. "Going to that diner for one; for another, dating someone outside my league." He snorted. "I just burned myself right there."

"Help me with her," Addy said, standing up and grabbing one of the girl's arms.

"Get off me!" Silvia shrieked, struggling as Travis did the same.

"E-" Addy said, holding out her other hand. Eli did not want to take it.

"Let me go!" the girl insisted.

"Let's go home," Addy said, staring hard at Eli. Eli did not want her eyes to turn red again, so he took her hand.

Travis looked at them. "Ready? Three, two, one." They all closed their eyes.

~

"Let me go!"

Eli opened his eyes to find himself and the other three right in front of Mia and Harper, who were still sitting on the couch. Addy dropped Eli and Silvia's hands and turned to Silvia, who tried to pull free of Travis's grip, but he grabbed her other hand so that she faced him.

"Listen, it's going to be okay," he assured her gently. "You just don't understand what's going on yet."

"What in the world! Who is *she?*" Mia asked, standing up and staring at Silvia.

"Um…" Travis's face blanched.

"It's kinda hard to explain," Addy said.

"She got shot, and when she woke up, she couldn't remember anything," Travis blurted. "We couldn't leave her."

"Leave her where?" Mia asked sharply.

"And why are you holding her hands?" Harper asked, her sharp eyes going from Travis's hands to his concerned face.

"Um…" Travis hastily dropped Silvia's hands. The girl backed up and turned as if she were about to bolt, but Mia intervened.

"It's okay," she said soothingly. "So, you just came across her shot?" Mia asked Travis hotly.

"Um…" He looked at Addy. "What happened with your eyes back there?" he asked, obviously trying to change the subject.

"What?" Addy asked.

"They glowed red, and you burned that dude's head off!"

Now everyone's eyes moved to Addy.

"I don't know," she told them. "I just felt hot and mad at whoever threatened Eli. And the girl sounded scared."

"Stop changing the subject!" Mia interjected. She paused,

thinking for a moment. "Travis, you dare?" She looked at Travis, indignant but impressed.

He looked down. "Yeah," he said quietly. "We have been together two years."

"Two years!" Mia exclaimed in shock. "You *dared*?"

"Um…yes," Travis said, looking at Silvia with sad eyes.

"Who are you?" Mia asked the baffled girl.

"I don't know!" Silvia answered desperately. "Who are you guys? This is all so strange."

"I know how you feel," Eli said, stepping forward. "Earlier today I woke up knowing nothing about my life, either."

She looked at Eli in wonder. "What?"

"I have a theory," Eli said, looking around the group. "I don't have much of an idea of what we are up against. But I think that somehow when one of us gets shot by those madmen, our memory is erased to make us turn on each other or to make us weak."

Mia raised her eyebrows. "Since when did you have a logical mind?"

"I don't know," he answered. His heart leapt as he looked at her, despite her grudging feelings towards him.

Harper stepped forward. "Who is she, Travis?"

The girl's frightened eyes bounced from Travis to Harper.

"Silvia, she… She's not in our league," Travis said, looking sadly at his confused girlfriend.

"What's going on here?"

All the teenagers jumped and turned to see Gideon approaching with a young woman following close behind. Eli stepped back at his brother's anger.

Mia started, "Um, Travis, Addy, and Eli just-"

Harper continued, "Appeared right in front of us with"

"No!" Travis blurted out.

Gideon's eyes shot to the strange girl. "Who is she? Who broke the rules? Who betrayed us?" Gideon barked, his sharp teeth bared in anger.

"No one betrayed us," Addy said, stepping forward. "We ran into this girl, and she seems to have lost her memory, like Eli."

"My brother did not lose his memory! He is just pretending. Speaking of which, I need to have a serious conversation with him. I will be right back to deal with *you*." Gideon glared at Silvia before turning back to the group. "Everyone, stay where you are. Don't let the intruder get away. Eli, come."

The buff guy turned on his heels. Eli didn't budge. Gideon looked over his shoulder. "Do not defy me again! *Come!*" He reached over and grabbed Eli by his shirt and started pulling him down the hall. The woman hustled after them while the others watched them go.

They reached the large circular room where Eli had first seen his brother. Gideon marched in a circle and approached him, fists clenched. "I've had enough of your pranks, Eli!"

"Pranks?"

"It's prank after prank, failed mission after failed mission! I will not allow you to bring the team down!"

"Um…I honestly have no idea what you are talking about," Eli said, desperately trying to get Gideon to see he was telling the truth.

"Stop it. Stop it! How many times do I have to tell you? Now, what went wrong?" Gideon loomed over Eli in anger.

"I-I don't know," Eli stuttered.

"You always say that," Gideon spat. He moved closer to Eli, who shrank back. "Now, what happened, and what is the story behind the new girl?"

Eli started to shake. Who was this person who seemed to hate him? And why was he so mad?

"Man, I don't know what's happening." Eli looked down at his trembling hand. "Seriously? *Seriously?* You think now is a good time to play a prank?"

"What is a prank? I have no clue-"

"Don't make me give you detention!"

"Detention?"

Gideon squeezed his eyes shut, opened them, and looked disappointed that Eli was still in front of him. "Listen, you ruined the attack yesterday; you didn't need to ruin the attack today, too. Did you pop the tire again? Mold Mia's nunchuck in clay? What did you decide to do?"

Eli felt like he was being looked at by hundreds of eyes instead of just two. "Brother? You are my brother, right? That's what M-Mia told me."

Gideon straightened his shoulders and stared coldly at Eli. "Stop it." Eli withered a little in his body. "Well?"

"You told me not to talk… To stop it?"

"I told you to stop pretending!"

Eli's eyes widened in fright. "Pretending what?"

"Pretending that you don't know anything! Gosh!" Gideon turned in an exasperated circle.

The woman approached Gideon as he put his hands to his head in anger. "Gideon, take it easy on him; he is younger than you, after all," she said.

Gideon softened slightly as the woman spoke. She put her hand soothingly on his shoulder. Eli watched both of them, his heart beating furiously as if he had just sprinted.

"Who are you?" Eli asked.

Gideon's fists clenched, but the woman stepped forward. "I'm Norah. Now, do you remember who you are?"

Eli stayed still. "Umm…"

"I've had enough!" Gideon bellowed.

"Gideon," Norah said gently. Eli shrank to the floor, staring up at Gideon and Norah, his eyes wide. Norah bent down to look him in the face.

"What is our mission here?" She asked Eli softly. Eli's gaze flitted to Norah's calm expression.

"I don't fully know, and I don't understand what's going on."

"You can't believe him, Norah. He is pretending!" Gideon insisted.

Norah stood up and looked at Gideon. "You seem so sure that he is faking, but look at him." She gestured to Eli, who cowered on the ground, watching the two argue. "He never acts like this, never this frightened."

"You could fool me. Remember the time-"

"This is not that time."

"Norah, he's pranked nearly every single person in this base at least once, if not dozens of times. How can this be any different?"

"Look at him!" Norah finally raised her voice.

Eli got the courage to get to his feet. "Please, I don't know what-" Eli stopped, unsure of what to say.

"See?" Norah gestured towards Eli. "He doesn't know."

Gideon's muscles stiffend. "I never thought I would see you side with Eli."

"I'm not *siding* with Eli. I'm just showing you that something different happened this time. He is not faking this. He really lost his memory. Something happened."

"Did Mia slap you or something?" Gideon asked Eli.

"Umm, she did slap me…" Eli admitted.

Gideon looked satisfied. "There. That settles it. Now spill what went wrong!"

Eli looked at Gideon indignantly. "No - no, I remember, um, waking up in a car and…that's it, honest. I don't know what happened before that. Mia didn't slap me until long after that."

"You don't remember my pep talk to your group?" Gideon asked.

Norah butted in, "You don't remember your last prank on Mia that you did this morning? She made a ruckus so loud it woke up half the building."

"…no, I don't," Eli told them.

Gideon looked like he wished that he could vaporize Eli on

the spot with his stare. He threw his hands up in exasperation.

"Gideon," Norah started, but Gideon turned sharply and stormed over to an intercom near the door.

"Mia!" Gideon bellowed, slamming the button with his finger. His voice boomed all around them. "Mia, come down here now!"

In an instant, Mia appeared. "Yes, Gideon?"

"Eli is refusing to tell me what happened on the mission, so you must tell me."

Mia glanced at Eli. Her anger at him seemed to have fizzled out...for now. "Um, you pretty much know. He got shot, the car crashed. When I woke him up, he acted dazed, he told them his name and now... I think I can show you something to prove that Eli doesn't know what's going on." She walked to the intercom. "Travis. Bring your, um...friend."

Silence. After a few moments, Travis led Silvia into the room. Gideon glared so hard at Travis that his eyes sparkled. Literally.

"Who is that?" he snarled at Travis.

Travis faltered, as if he might pass out. "She's um... she's-"

"A friend," Mia butted in. Travis looked at Mia with a questioning look.

"From where? I know everyone in our league. She is not in our league." Gideon stormed over to Silvia, who backed up in fright. "Who are you, exactly?"

"I don't know!" Silvia said. She looked at Travis with pleading eyes.

"*I don't know,*" Gideon mimicked in a high-pitched voice that, in Eli's opinion, should not have been able to come out of such a buff guy. Then, he snapped back to his anger. "Leagues may not visit each other. This is against the law. This means execution!"

Travis gasped. "No! You can't!" He ran over to Silvia, pulling her to his chest.

Silvia struggled. "What? I don't understand! What's going on?" Silvia cried.

"That's what I would like to know!" Gideon demanded.

"I think we're all confused about what is going on today," Mia butted in again. "You can't kill her, Gideon."

"Watch me!" Right before Eli's eyes, Gideon transformed into a large, hairy beast with the same teeth he had flashed at Eli earlier. The strange creature arched its back and bared its fangs.

"Gideon, no! *Stop!*" Mia ran towards the creature, but it leaped over Mia, who then ran right into Eli. They both crashed to the floor, Mia landing right on top of him.

"Hey," he said, staring into Mia's eyes.

Mia ferociously pushed herself up and off Eli and in one brisk movement turned to face Gideon. Eli sat up to see Gideon circling Travis and Silvia. Travis clung to Silvia, her back to his chest, turning so that his back faced Gideon's fangs.

"What's happening?" the girl squeaked out, trying to get out of Travis's protective grip while also trying to get away from Gideon.

Eli got to his feet, stunned. What in the world has Gideon become?

"Gideon, stop!" Mia screamed. An angry tear slid down her face. She took the device with two black handles connected by a silver chain out of her pocket and ran to stand between Gideon and Travis, trying to protect Silvia.

Gideon's eyes flared yellow, and he leaped towards Travis. Mia lunged to intercept the attack, and Gideon squealed a terrible un-Gideon-like squeal as the black part of Mia's weapon smacked him on the head.

The furry creature fell mid-jump and landed on the floor as the buff young adult once again. Blood trickled from Gideon's head. Silvia had stopped struggling to free herself and buried her face in Travis's shoulder, sobbing from fright.

"Why do you care about me so much? I don't know you!" Silvia cried.

Mia's face turned pale as she saw the damage she had caused. She rushed over to Gideon and knelt next to him. Eli rushed to her side, wanting to help.

"What happened?" Eli asked.

"You saw, didn't you, idiot?" Mia snapped, brushing away a tear.

Gideon stirred and groaned.

Norah rushed over to Gideon's side and turned to Mia. "You," she snapped. "You and Eli are always causing trouble."

"I don't! It's always Eli!"

"Hey!" Eli protested.

"Stop it!" Norah roared.

Gideon sat up groggily, rubbing his head.

"You okay, honey?" the woman asked soothingly. Eli stared at the woman in shock. *Honey? This woman cannot possibly be Gideon's girlfriend, can she?*

"Norah," Gideon groaned. He opened his eyes.

"Oh, thank goodness!" she exclaimed. She placed her hand on top of Gideon's head where the cut was and slowly spread out her fingers. When she removed her hand, the cut was perfectly healed.

"How did you -" Eli started to ask.

"Her blessing. Healing power," Mia whispered to Eli.

Gideon shook his head. "Get the girl away from Travis. We need to talk to her," Gideon ordered, shaken from his injury.

"Mia, we'll talk later," Norah said as she approached Travis and Silvia. "Come with me," she said coldly to Silvia.

Silvia looked up. "Why should I go with you?" she asked. "I don't know you. I don't know anyone. I don't even know who I am." She looked like she might cry again.

"Gideon," Travis said, letting go of Silvia and stepping towards his leader. "She had information on the gold brick."

Gideon stood up so fast that the blood drained from his face. "What?"

"Um…" Travis glanced uneasily at Silvia, who looked completely baffled.

"What was it? Why didn't you tell me sooner?" Gideon's fangs flashed in and out of sight again.

"Um, stuff happend so fast," Travis said.

"I know what happened… I think," Eli said, stepping forward.

Gideon turned on him sharply. "You what? What happened?"

"I was at, um, a restaurant with Addy. I saw Travis but didn't remember who he was…" Eli continued to recount his chaotic date. "And so now they know whatever it was Silvia knew," he finished. He swallowed what little saliva had accumulated in his mouth.

"What did you tell them?" Gideon asked, turning crisply on

the frightened girl.

She took a step back. "I don't know," she said.

"Gideon, I have an idea," Eli said, walking over between Travis and Silvia.

Gideon glared at his brother. "What?"

"I think the bullets, um, somehow make the person they shot forget everything. They erase their memory to maybe make them turn on their own team, err, league."

Gideon studied Eli, arms folded. "That's an interesting thought, brother."

Eli flinched. He did not like the thought that this buff, grumpy guy was his brother. No. He did not like it at all.

"Thanks," Eli said.

"So now what?" Travis asked.

Norah seemed to realize she was not obeying Gideon. She jerked Silvia to her side and pulled both the girl's arms behind her back as if she were going to tie her wrists together.

"Let me go!" Silvia shrieked. Travis's body jerked with the impulse to release Silvia from Norah's grip.

"Clear out!" Gideon roared. "I want everyone but Eli and this girl to leave! Mia — room detention for attacking me!"

"But—" Mia started to protest.

"Go!"

"You were going to kill someone!" Mia insisted, storming up to him as her hair bounced up and down in a dazzling way. She was nose-to-nose with Gideon now, and Eli realized just how brave Mia was.

"Fraternizing with the enemy, who knows what he told her," Gideon spat.

Travis started forward angrily but stopped himself.

"I feel like you're my parent even though you're not," Mia grumbled, storming out of the room. Norah shoved Silvia away and turned to follow her, leaving just Gideon, Silvia, Travis, and Eli in the room.

"Travis, go," Gideon ordered.

"No," Travis countered, his voice shaking.

"You will go *now*."

"You will not kill her," Travis said stubbornly.

"We'll see," Gideon said unconvincingly.

Travis glanced at Silvia, then ran out of the room.

"So. What's the real story behind this?" Gideon asked.

"What I told you," Eli said again, stepping forward.

Gideon looked to Silvia, who shrank back in fright. "What happened to you today?" Gideon asked her.

"I don't know! I woke up and was surrounded by strangers," Silvia said. "They somehow got me here and now —

I don't know!" She burst out crying.

"Stop blubbering," Gideon snapped.

Silvia stepped back, shaking.

"Dude. She lost her memory, like me," Eli said.

"I don't believe you. This is all one big prank you cooked up," Gideon said. "I'll give you the night to sleep on it, then we will have a meeting. Leave me."

Eli took a step back. "What are you going to do with Silvia?" he asked.

Gideon glared at her. His fangs flashed again. "She'll go to jail for now, until we figure out what to do with her."

She shrank back, wiping her eyes. "Jail?" she asked.

"Eli, go to your room," Gideon said in a tone not to be disobeyed.

Eli walked away, confused by everything that had happened that day and wondering what would be coming next.

~

Eli walked into his "new" room and slammed the door.

"Hey." Eli jumped, having completely forgotten about his roommate, Bryce. "So… How'd it go? Are you crazy in love with Addy yet?"

"What?" With all the excitement, Eli had forgotten all about his date with Addy. "Um…"

Bryce sat up and leaned against the rail of the bunk bed. "You okay, bro?"

"Oh...well, it kinda backfired on me." He stopped and snorted as he realized what he had said.

"What?"

"Um...there was an incident. I don't even know if I can explain it in a way I could make sense of. Especially for you."

"What happened?" Bryce asked eagerly.

"Well, I met Travis."

"Hey! You and him are - er, were? - great friends!" Bryce said, swinging his legs over the ladder and climbing down.

"Yeah. Apparently, we are good friends — but we ran into another friend of his..."

"Who? Mia? Harper? You already know them, dude. Stop messing with me."

"Um...we met a new friend, someone outside our base — a girl."

Bryce was so surprised that he fell off the remaining rungs. "Excuse me, what?" He picked himself up as Eli sat in his swivel chair.

"You might want to sit down."

"You think?" Bryce asked, rubbing the lump that had formed on his head.

Eli repeated the story of his date.

"Um, you're telling me Travis has been cheating on us?" Bryce asked incredulously.

"Um…" Eli scooted his chair back at the emotion in Bryce's voice.

"I mean — cheating on our league? He's been betraying us, and who knows how much of our information he has passed to *her* league."

"I don't think it was like that. She's in jail now anyway," Eli said.

"What! A strange girl from a different league is in this building? What are we waiting for? Let's go find her!"

"Bryce, stop!" Eli protested. Bryce bounded out the door, bouncing on the balls of his feet. "A moment ago, you were saying that she was sneaking information to her side and - hey!"

But Bryce was racing down the hall. "C'mon!"

"But… Oh, whatever!" Eli ran after Bryce.

Chapter 4

"Are you crazy?" Eli gasped. He had finally caught up with Bryce, who stood outside a metal door.

"Yup! Pretty girl, here I come!"

"Dude, she's Travis' girlfriend."

"Should that stop me?" Bryce opened the metal door and surveyed the room. It was metal like the rest, and in it were four cells. Each had a sink, a toilet, and a wooden cot. The lights were dim, but one flickered, threatening to go out.

In the far-left cell was Silvia. She had scrunched herself into a corner, her whole body trembling.

"And here I come," Bryce hissed to Eli.

"Dude, you can't—"

Their whispers had caught Silvia's attention. Her tear-streaked face looked up, and she spotted the two boys.

"Hey," Bryce said, walking in an un-Bryce-like way up to the bars of her cell. She stared first at him, then at Eli. Her eyes were red from crying, and her curly hair danced in a pattern all over her face. She was still really pretty, even with her messy hair and muddy clothes.

"So, how's it going?" Bryce asked, leaning casually against the bars.

"Dude, how thick can you get?" Eli asked, staring at Bryce.

Just then, the door banged open, and Travis slammed into the room. He ran for the cell and fell on his knees, clenching his fists around two bars like he wanted to pull the bars straight off the cell.

"Silvia! Are you okay?" He seemed not to notice that he had interrupted Bryce flirting with his girlfriend.

Silvia's gaze moved to Travis. "I don't know where I am or who I am," she said.

"I know who you are. You are Silvia Clark, you are in League Two, and your parents are Edward and Trica. They both love fuzzy things. And you love music."

Silvia's eyes dove deep into Travis's. Bryce backed up, causing Silvia to break eye contact with Travis. Travis looked around. His face changed at the sight of Bryce.

"What are yo-" He noticed Eli.

"Um. Hi," Eli said awkwardly.

"What are you doing? Were you trying to take my girl?" Travis sprang up and turned toward Bryce.

"Well, we don't get many new ones in here, do we?" Bryce asked defensively.

"No! But you don—"

"Guys!" Eli shouted. The two arguing teens turned to Eli.

"Do I know you? Because you don't seem to be the Eli I remember," Travis said.

"Um, I don't think I am. But how should I know?"

"What's going on here?" Harper asked as she walked into the room. Her eyes drank in the sight of the angry boys and terrified girl. Bryce flushed slightly.

"That's a good question," Travis said, turning to Eli. "What are either of you doing here?"

"Um…I told Bryce about what happened, and he came straight here…" Eli explained.

Travis glared at Bryce.

"Dude, you know how few girls come through here—" Bryce's ears were bright red.

"Just shut up!" Eli bellowed. Everyone stared at him.

"C'mon, guys," Eli reasoned. "We're a team, right? Sure, I feel like I've only known you all for less than a day, even though I supposedly have known you all for years, but still! We need to find a way to get the brick, right? We won't get anywhere by arguing."

"Eli's right. And I'm completely confused as to why you're all here," Harper added.

Eli shrugged. "It doesn't matter."

"Why are *you* here?" Travis asked ferourshously.

"Looking for Bryce."

"What matters is that we trust one another," Eli said. "We're all we've got."

"When did you get wise and all-knowing?" Travis asked, folding his arms.

"I don't know," Eli admitted.

"Poor Eli," Harper said. "But maybe this Silvia knows something."

"We know she *knew* something," Travis said. He turned to Silvia. "What do you remember?" he asked, kneeling once again by the bars.

Her wide eyes roamed over the group.

"Hey, it's okay," Bryce said.

"Dudes, maybe you should all clear out. This might be a girl-to-girl conversation," Harper said.

"Good idea!" Eli jumped in, desperate to break the tension between Travis and Bryce. Eli walked over to the two disgruntled teens and pushed them out of the room, shutting the metal door behind him as he did. When they were outside, Travis and Bryce faced each other angrily.

"You—" Travis began.

"Does it really matter that much?" Eli interrupted Travis.

"But—" Bryce started.

Eli interrupted again, "Minutes ago, you were saying how Travis was betraying us and that Silvia would be gathering information from us and relaying that information to the enemy, and now—"

"What? You think I would betray you?" Travis yelled at Bryce.

"Well, not anymore," Bryce said sheepishly.

"You're just trying to get her on your good side. Well, too bad for you, bud, she has Travis, so lay off," Eli said. Bryce folded his arms.

Travis went on, "I would never betray our team, thank you very much. Do you want me to go to her side and—"

"No!" Bryce cut in. "I… I was being stupid."

"Yes, you were!"

"Okay. Now that's settled. I have an idea." But before Eli could elaborate, Harper came out of the jail.

"Any luck?" Travis asked.

"No. Just the same 'I don't know who I am. I don't know where I am.'"

"That's what happened to me, I keep telling you," Eli insisted.

"What do we do with her?" Bryce asked.

"*You* will do nothing with her," Travis told Bryce. Bryce huffed.

"We can't take her back to her league; she knows too much about us," Harper said.

Travis brightened. "Then I think we have someone new on our side!"

"But then she will be betraying her team," Eli put in.

"Do we have a choice? We have to welcome her as one of us," Harper said.

"Like Gideon is going to go for that." Bryce scoffed.

"Well…" Harper paused. "What else is there to do? Her memory is fully gone. She's scared and has no idea where she is. She's a mess, too. She should get herself cleaned up."

"No kidding," Bryce muttered.

"Hey—" Travis started to argue with Bryce, but Harper interrupted him.

"I'll go get Gideon."

"No! He'll throw another fit! He'll… he'll…" Travis started to protest, but Harper was already gone. "I'm toast. Okay, maybe a roast."

"Well done or rare?" Bryce asked, but all he received was a stony look from Travis.

A few minutes later, Harper returned, Gideon with her. He

glared at the group.

"I've had enough of you for one day, Eli. As for this girl, fine. Let her out. Just don't you dare let her out of this building. And you"—he turned to Travis— "behave yourself."

Gideon stormed past them into the jail. Silence rested on the group for a few moments, then Gideon shoved Silvia out and thrust her toward Harper. He slammed the door to the jail and turned on the group. "Harper is in charge of that—"

"Her name's Silvia," Travis butted in.

Gideon glared at him. "One more toe out of line, and you are a pork chop. Meeting in two hours. One minute late, and there will be severe punishment." Gideon left.

Harper's voice broke the silence. "Well, c'mon, Silvia. I'll show you to the showers."

Silvia gave Harper a blank expression. Her eyes were red, tear streaks glistening on her cheeks.

Travis stepped forward. "Silvia. I... I'm glad you are going to be welcomed into our league."

Bryce snorted. "Welcomed? I think it was more of—"

Eli jabbed Bryce in the ribs.

"Let's go," Eli said.

"C'mon, Silvia. Let me show you your new home." Harper grabbed Sivlia's hand and led her away.

Chapter 5

Two hours later, the group gathered at a long office table lined with swivel chairs.

There were dozens of people scattered inside the room. The table had triangle name plaques by each chair, indicating where people should sit. Eli sat down at his spot and looked around. People were milling about, talking, laughing, and sending uneasy glances towards Silvia. Bryce, Travis, Mia, and Addy sat down at Eli's right, and to his left, Harper sat next to the newcomer. When Harper had entered the room leading Silvia, she had no problem winding her way through people; the others had immediately felt the presence of an unfamiliar person and parted without request, eyeing Silvia as if she were acid.

"So, how's everything going?" Eli muttered to Harper.

"Gre- "

Gideon cut Harper off as he flung the doors open and strutted into the room with Norah. "Everyone to your places!" he barked.

"You're two seconds late!" a boy called out. He was short with a child-like voice, but his features indicated that he was around fifteen.

"Be quiet, Kace!" Gideon growled.

The boy, Kace, looked down but kept on grinning. Everyone, young and old, rushed to their spots. They were mostly young people, but a few were older and in wheelchairs, missing limbs or using crutches. The oldest one looked about seventy. There were a few murmured conversations that flitted between people. A girl with pink hair smiled and waved at Eli. He gave a tentative wave and an unsure smile back. Gideon sat at the end of the table, and Norah sat at his right. The other end of the table was empty.

"Okay, everyone," Gideon commanded, "listen up. We have a report on how the raid went." Silence filled the room. Gideon looked at Mia. "Mia will give us the details of what went wrong."

Her face flushed, and Eli felt anger surging, that Gideon would make Mia tell what had happened, when it had been *his* fault, according to her. Mia stood up.

"Everything was going well," she said. "We had made it halfway to League One. But we had miscalculated. There was a scout from League Three who came down 94th Street in a snowplow. He somehow knew that our car was not friendly and started chasing us. Other men from League Three fired at the car. A bullet made contact with Eli, and he collapsed."

Eli's face turned beet-red as people stared at him in a disapproving way as if to say, *How weak. How could you pass out after being shot?*

"I was driving," Mia continued, her hair rocking back and forth slightly as she turned her head to look at everyone in the room. "He had been fending off the men from League Three. I was distracted when the window shattered. The car ran into a stoplight. I got him to wake up, but he was severely dazed."

Eli looked down, face feeling like a burning stovetop.

"I got him out of the car and into an alley. But there was a problem. A man started chasing us." Eli looked up and made eye contact with Mia. *Is she blushing?* Eli thought, hopefully. She looked away and started talking again. "I dragged him down the alley, and he seemed to be playing a prank on me, acting stupid. That's what I thought at first, but he was even more of a dufus than he had been before. The man caught up to me and - and, um..." She cleared her throat. "He grabbed Eli from behind and started choking him. The others"—she motioned to Bryce, Layla, and Harper— "came and helped me free him. Eli claimed that he could not remember any of us, and we brought him back here. And that's the end."

She sat down. Intense silence followed Mia's speech.

"Eli, would you like to testify?" Gideon asked. All heads turned to face Eli. He felt like a tiny crumb. He looked to Bryce.

"You have to, dude," Bryce hissed.

Eli stood up, shaking. "Um...I did lose my memory," he said. Murmuring filled the room, Eli plowed on regardless. "I don't remember any of you. The only people I know are the ones I've re-met today."

The girl who had waved at him looked startled. Her name tag read *Kayla.*

"I only know what Bryce or the others have told me," Eli finished. He took his seat.

People seemed restless. Eli noticed that the person sitting next to Silvia had inched his chair away from her as if she were something contagious.

Gideon nodded. "I'm not sure that I am buying Eli's story, but—"

"You can't ignore two people's testimonies that line up," Bryce interrupted. "I was there, and so were Layla and Harper. We can all agree he seemed dazed."

"You can say that again," Mia said.

Gideon glared at them. "Thank you for your famous input there. Now. I will address the brick in the room."

Everyone turned to stare at Silvia, who shrank back. She had cleaned up; her hair was brushed and pulled back into a low ponytail, and she had changed clothes.

"We have had an...um, unfortunate turn of events." Gideon glanced at Travis. "Eli, I think it's your turn to tell the story."

Eli gawked at his brother. He shrank down in his seat, trying to be invisible. To his bewilderment, Addy stood up, drawing everyone's attention away from him. Eli breathed again.

"I was going on a date with Eli," she said. There were some snickers, and some boys Eli did not know looked over at him. "We went to a restaurant." Several women gasped and shot disapproving looks at the two.

"We ran into Travis," Addy continued as Travis started and dropped his head like he had dropped a pen. "He was with another girl. Silvia."

More people murmured. Travis continued to stare at the ground.

"Anyways. The men from League Three grabbed Eli and threatened to kill him unless someone who had a lead on how to break League One stepped forward. Silvia said she had a lead. They took her out of the restaurant, and I don't know what happened. The next thing we knew, there were two gunshots, and the men came back into the restaurant. One of them told everyone in his league to leave, and they did so. Eli and I left, along with Travis. We found Silvia outside in a corner, unconscious. When she woke up, she had no idea who she was or who Travis was. We took her back to base, and now here we are."

An old man stood up and spoke in a shaky voice, breaking through the murmurs. "How do we know she is not a spy?"

"Because she acted the same as I did when I woke up. Well,

almost," Eli said, sitting up and glancing at Mia.

"She could not, does not—um...remember who I am," Travis said.

"Is that a problem?" a woman asked, looking at Travis skeptically.

"If she is from a different league, how do you know her?" another voice asked.

Suddenly the whole table was grilling Travis with questions he clearly did not want to answer.

"How long have you known her?"

"Are you two dating?"

"Did you betray us?"

"Did you two have your first kiss?" a tiny voice asked.

"Quiet!" Gideon roared. Everyone sat back in their seats and looked at Gideon. "Let's let her talk." He looked over to Silvia, who shrank even further. "What do you remember happening today?"

Silvia looked terrified but, at a whisper from Harper, sat up straight.

"I..." Her voice shook. She glanced at Travis and seemed to regain some confidence. She cleared her throat. "I woke up in a disgusting place. Um...Travis, Addy, and Eli were surrounding me. I did not know who they were. They seemed concerned, and I had no idea why. They kept asking me things and talking gibberish to me. I could barely make sense of what they were saying. And, um…they brought me here. So…yeah." She huddled into her seat as the room went silent.

"How do we know you're telling the truth? How do we know that you're not a spy and that Travis and the others are in on this to get us all killed?" a muscle-bound boy asked.

Travis stood up in anger. "I would *never*—"

"This is supposed to be a civilized meeting," Gideon reminded everyone. People looked wary at Travis's anger, and several had drawn their weapons.

"Yeah! How do we know she's not at this meeting for other reasons?" a woman's shrill voice called out.

"Quiet!"

Everyone turned to Norah in shock. Her voice had sounded like a thunderclap. Now Eli understood why Gideon had taken a fancy to her.

"We are getting nowhere," Gideon complained. "What we need is to find a way to get into Base One so that we can get out of this mess."

"Fat chance," the elder said. "I have been here my whole life. My grandma before that even. No one is going to win anytime soon, if ever."

"Thank you for the encouraging comment, Fifi," Norah

said sarcastically.

Eli tentatively raised his hand. Everyone's attention focused on Eli once more.

"Yes, brother?" Gideon raised his eyebrows as he addressed Eli.

Eli flinched at being called *brother*.

"Um...I have an idea. It's crazy, and I still don't know much about what we are up against, but—" Eli glanced at Silvia. "I think I know how we can get the brick." Silence filled the room. "I think we need to work together."

Someone snorted. "We are. We have been working together for decades."

"No," Eli contradicted. "That's not what I mean. We have been working together, but *we*"—he looked pointedly at Silvia, then at the crowd— "*we* have not worked together. The leagues have always fought for themselves, right? What if we teamed up with Silvia's league and—"

"That's bonkers!"

"They'll betray us!"

"You are trying to betray us!"

"You care nothing for us!"

"Eli's right!" Mia's voice rang loud and clear in Eli's head. He looked at her gratefully.

"Stupid idea!"

"I'll never work!"

"It's against the rules."

Once everyone had quieted down, Eli looked nervously at his brother. Gideon wore an interesting expression, like he was contemplating, but also like he had just taken a bite of a lemon when he had expected chocolate.

"I stand with Eli as well," Harper said.

"Same here," Addy said.

Eli's ears turned red as a group of boys across the table started whispering to each other.

"Interesting idea, brother," Gideon said. He had his chin in his hand. "But it would never work."

Eli's face fell. "How do you know that?" he challenged.

Whispers and gasps rippled like water.

"Um, Eli, no one defies Gideon," Bryce whispered to Eli.

"Well, I do," Eli hissed back. "I don't care if he is my brother."

Gideon's gaze penetrated him. Those mysterious flames sparked in his eyes again. "You be quiet," he said silkily to Eli.

Eli looked down but clenched his fists. Then suddenly, Eli felt himself getting sleepy. He blinked hard and looked up at Gideon, who continued talking about something or another.

Eli had been through so much that day. He was so tired…so tired.

New friends, new love, new enemies…

So sleepy. He closed his eyes.

~

Eli opened his eyes with a start. Someone was shaking his shoulder. "Eli! Eli, c'mon."

"Mia?" he managed to say in his grogginess, sitting up and rubbing his eyes. Bryce was shaking his shoulder. He was still in the meeting room, but most people were milling about, leaving, or discussing different things in their chairs.

"Dude. You must be dead tired," Bryce said. "Let's get you back to our bunk."

"Wha?" Eli blinked hard and shook his head. Then he remembered the past few hours. He got up and stiffly shambled towards the door with Bryce. The girl with the pink hair, Kayla, bounded over to them.

"What's up, Eli?" she asked, falling into step beside him.

"Um…do I know you?"

"We had one mission together."

"Uh… Honestly, I don't know what's up," Eli said.

Kayla's face turned pale.

"Eli."

Eli jumped and looked up. Gideon and Norah, their arms crossed, were staring at him.

"Yes?" Eli asked.

"Talk later," Kayla whispered as she slipped away.

"You fell asleep during the meeting," Gideon said disapprovingly.

"Okay. I didn't mean to," Eli said, yawning a wide yawn.

"We will talk in the morning," Gideon stated. "We will discuss the next raid that you and the others will embark on. Without any mess-ups."

"Okay," Eli said unenthusiastically. "And my plan?"

"I'll think about it," Gideon responded.

~

Eli woke up with a start. The previous night, his head had hit the pillow like a bowling ball.

Bryce was shaking him awake. "Eli. C'mon. Gideon will be furious. You don't want to miss breakfast."

Eli sat up. "Where?"

"C'mon, c'mon!" Bryce insisted. Bryce was fully dressed, and Eli had fallen asleep in his clothes. Eli scrambled down the ladder and followed Bryce out the door. "If we miss breakfast, then we won't eat until noon!"

The two raced down the halls to a large cafeteria. Eli

followed Bryce's lead, piling his tray high with sausage, toast, eggs, and cheese. Bryce slid into a seat next to Harper and the other people that Eli had gotten to know a little the day before. Mia approached the table, but when she saw that the only available seat was next to Eli, she scowled and moved to another table.

"Why does she hate me again?" Eli asked Bryce as he stared after her.

"Well, for one, before yesterday, you were always pranking her," Bryce said.

"Is that a reason to be mad at someone?"

"Umm…"

"You came up with some clever ones," Addy piped up from the far end of the table.

"I did?"

"Yeah, like the time-"

"Okay. That's enough," Travis interrupted. Eli saw that Silvia wasn't at the table.

"Where's…?"

Travis seemed to have read Eli's mind. "Gideon forced her to spend the night in jail." His face had a bitter expression. "He said he didn't want to take any risks. Apparently, she's still there."

Just then, the door to the room banged open, and Norah dragged Silvia, handcuffed, into the cafeteria and grabbed a filled plate. Travis jumped to his feet, but Gideon appeared from nowhere and accosted him.

"You won't be going anywhere near her, traitor."

"I am not a traitor!" Travis defended himself.

"Oh, really? Only conversing with the enemy, only being with her for *two years,* doing who knows what with her, without telling anyone. Oh, no. You are no traitor," Gideon sarcastically drawled.

Both Addy and Harper stood up to restrain Travis from attacking Gideon head-on.

"Tsk tsk. I don't envy your role in today's siege." Gideon strolled   off.

"How can you let him be your leader?" Eli asked angrily. "How did he become our leader?"

"He came up with a plan that helped us get into League One's base. But half of our league died in that siege," Harper told him.

"Oh…"

"Time's up! Everyone to your usual tasks!" Gideon roared to the room. Everyone scrambled to obey. Once Eli's table had cleared their dishes away and scrubbed them clean, Mia joined the group. Eli thought she looked even prettier after she had showered and straightened her hair. He moved over to her.

"So, what's next?" he asked. She walked over to Harper and engaged in conversation. Eli sighed.

"Nice try," Bryce muttered to him.

"Thanks," Eli said unenthusiastically. "I'm thrilled that the one girl I like hates me. And I don't even remember why."

"It is a pity," Bryce agreed.

"It's worse to have your girlfriend totally forget you," Travis chimed in.

"The girl you were not supposed to have," Bryce grumbled.

"Hey. What can I say? Saw her in an attack and—"

"That's enough, I think," Eli butted in.

Gideon approached their table. "Come," Gideon said simply.

Eli looked at Bryce and Travis with raised eyebrows. The group followed Gideon through the room. Eli spotted Kayla, who waved merrily at him. Eli's eyes immediately drooped sleepily. He nodded. He started to collapse mid-stride when Travis and Bryce caught him under his arms.

"Woah, man," Bryce said. "Looks like you forgot how to fight Kayla's blessing."

"Huh?"

"She can make people sleep. To fight it, one must think of

caffeine, sugar, all that good stuff. She can't help but put people to sleep once in a while."

"Great. Just great," Eli said.

Gideon interrupted their conversation: "Enough talk. Now. Here is your task."

Chapter 6

Eli was *so* thrilled with the plan. He and his group were to approach League Two's base with Silvia and declare a truce. Eli would be leading the procession. *Great. Just great. Gideon takes my plan and makes me sacrifice myself to the league.*

"Man, if I don't make it out of this," Eli said to Bryce as they suited up in their room later, "I thank you for being on my side."

"No biggie, bro, we're like family here."

"Like family. Family that hates each other. Can't she give me a chance?"

"You haven't even told her that you like her, dude."

"She'll slit my throat if I do." Eli's stomach churned at the thought of telling Mia what he had been feeling deep down, the feeling he had been trying to push away ever since Bryce had told him that he was the bravest person he had ever met.

"Mia's right. You've seriously changed."

"What?" Eli's brain woke up. "When did you talk to her?"

"After you crashed in bed last night. I went for a walk and ran into her."

"What else did she say?" Eli asked as the two left their room.

Bryce remained silent. They met the others: Travis, Mia, Harper, Layla, Silvia - still in handcuffs - and Gideon by the league's entranceway.

"Ready?" Gideon asked the group, setting his face.

"No," Eli said. "I'm not ready to die."

Layla stifled a snicker.

"Okay, let's go," Mia said, looking serious.

"Oh, and Travis," Gideon said, catching his arm. Travis looked at Gideon. "Don't fail me again. Or..." His teeth flashed sharp, then back to normal.

Travis gulped. "I'm honored that you have let me live this long." He flinched at what he just said.

Gideon glared at him, then let him go. "Off with you now."

"Ready?" Harper asked. She grabbed Mia's hand, and Mia grabbed Layla's hand.

Layla reached for Travis's hand.

Eli raised his eyebrows at them. "We're going to be holding hands?" he asked. He was disappointed that he was not near Mia.

"No, dummy," Mia said. "Just to get there."

"So, appear right in the middle of their base? Won't that cause a ruckus? So much for a *we come in peace* tribute, whatever that means."

Mia rolled her eyes. "That would result in almost instantaneous death, nitwit. We will appear *outside* their base. We're not stupid."

"Umm..."

"People have tried that before... They never came back," Bryce whispered to Eli. Eli's stomach dropped.

"Okay, let's focus," Mia ordered.

Once they were in a semicircle, they all closed their eyes. When Eli opened them again, he was squinting in the sunlight, and a large fortress loomed before them.

~

Rows of guards in armor surrounded the fortress every few feet. When they saw the teenagers appear, they readied their guns and aimed them at the teens.

"The white flag—the flag, Eli!" Mia pressed a white rag into his hands. He looked back at the group behind him. Bryce nodded encouragingly, looking like he was about to be sick. Eli swallowed hard and stepped forward. Immediately the guards stepped forward as well and cocked their guns as one.

"The flag, nitwit!" Mia's tight voice came from behind him.

Eli held up the flag.

None of the guards moved a centimeter.

"Silvia," Mia whispered. "Travis, bring her."

"But—"

"You heard Gideon," Mia prompted. Eli heard Travis step forward. The clicking of handcuffs told Eli that Silvia had moved closer to him. A movement disturbed the line of guards. Someone came pelting out of the building, causing the guards to start.

"Silvia! *Silvia!*" A woman who looked like Silvia came tearing out of the building, tears streaming down her face. The guards moved to block her from reaching the group.

Eli continued to hold the flag up. "We come in peace," he said loudly to the yard.

The woman fought the guard's grip. "That's my daughter, *you!* She has been missing! Silvia!" The woman's cries were gut-wrenching to hear.

"Trica," Travis whispered. The woman looked like an identical twin of Silvia but thirty years older.

"Um...we come to make a truce," Eli said lamely.

"Let my daughter go!" Trica screamed at the group. She wrenched free from the guards and ran for her daughter. Silvia shrank back. Travis intercepted the woman, and the guards started forward, ready to defend their league's own.

"Stop," he told the woman.

"You stop!" Trica countered.

"No, listen. I'm her boyfriend. I would never let anything bad happen to her."

With this, the woman stepped back and nearly fainted dead away. "What's this?" she gasped.

A man broke ranks from the building and ran for the group. The guards once more intervened, stopping the man in his tracks. "Let me get to them! Let me avenge my daughter!" the man snarled.

Just then, the guards stiffened, and they parted, leaving a clear walkway. A tall black man in a purple cloak emerged from the building. An old-fashioned sword dangled at his waist, with a modern-day pistol on the other side. He walked slowly, studying the group of pathetic-looking teens. Eli moved the banner to cover his face. Mia hissed and punched him in the back.

"What is this? No guns drawn?" he drawled, stopping a few feet away from the group of unfamiliar warriors.

"No," Mia said, then whispered to Eli. "Go on."

Eli put the flag down, and trembling, stepped forward. "Um. We come in peace," he squeaked out.

"Oh, forget it," he heard Mia grumble. She strode in front of him. "We come in peace!" she proclaimed to the group at large. Some of the guards stepped back in shock.

"Strange, coming from the people who kidnapped one of

my allies," the leader of League Two drawled out.

"We did not mean to steal her!" Travis butted in, stepping forward. "She lost her memory! We could not leave her on the streets to be killed!"

"Travis," Eli muttered.

"Oh. So, you care about us?" League Two's leader asked. "How surprising. I don't know how many times your league has maimed and injured our league."

"We have a truce we wish to declare," Mia interrupted. The leader's hand inched towards his sword as Mia got closer.

Eli's stomach felt like a fist had clenched over it. *How could I let her go by herself?*

But those guns were still out, and they were big. "Truce? After all these years, you are sacrificing yourselves to us?"

"No." A ripple went through the guards. Silvia's mom had retreated to where her husband was being restrained, watching the group with widening eyes. "We have an idea on how to get the brick."

The leader took a step back. "And you are asking for our help?" he asked.

"Yes, in a way."

"They're bargaining!" Silvia's dad claimed. "They are trying to get us on their good side because they have my daughter! They want to learn our secrets and then betray us!"

Silvia's eyes were fixed on the two people who seemed to care for her so much, but her eyes did not register any recognition.

"Quiet, fool," the leader growled. Travis started forward, but Harper stopped him. "Well, I guess I am willing to hear your so-called plan before we attack and get our league back together."

"We never said we were giving her back!" Layla piped up.

"L! Stop," Harper intervened.

"I see you brought famous Eli with you," the leader observed. Everyone started and stared at Eli.

"How?" he started to ask, but then he understood. No doubt those other men would have spread his name far and wide just to get him killed.

"A little voice told me."

"Never mind about that now," Mia butted in. "We have a plan but don't want to announce it to the world. May we speak in private?"

"Only if your team leaves behind all weapons."

Eli looked to Mia, who had turned to her team, face deadly pale. "We have to," she said sullenly.

"M—"

"Drop all weapons!" Mia said as if it pained her to say it. Eli fished in his pockets and dropped what he had brought. The clatter of weapons hitting the ground churned Eli's stomach into a ball of anger.

"Good," the leader of League Two said.

"And you? Are you going to drop your weapons?"

"No. I think not. You will be intruding in our league, after all. Come."

The group walked forward, their muscles tense, through the group of guards, and into the main entrance. It appeared to be exactly like theirs.

"Silvia!" Trica called out. Silvia hardly glanced at her. Once the door had slid shut, and they were safely — well, maybe not *safely* — enclosed in the entrance area, the leader turned to the group.

"So, you are choosing to barter with us, eh? Silvia, get over here."

Silvia made eye contact with him. "I don't know who you are."

He looked startled at her refusal. "Silvia, stop playing."

Layla hid a snicker, obviously thinking of Mia's initial thoughts from the day before when Eli had woken up.

"She is not playing," Travis said hotly, stepping forward.

"Enough, T," Mia snapped. "Eli, you are the one who had

the idea."

Eli swallowed. "Um. Sir." He gave an awkward bow, and Layla snorted again. "I had an idea. No one has succeeded in decades."

"Obviously."

"But." Eli wiped the sweat off his face. It was so warm in this building. "But no one has ever worked together — as in, more than one league working together to get the brick."

"Foolishness. We can't."

"Who said we couldn't work together, huh?" A surge of courage swept through him. He had never felt anything like this. "Have you heard of a time when someone said, 'Oh, no one can work together. They'll die if they do.' It's not like the leagues haven't tried to get the brick for decades, and no one has succeeded alone. Or if you like, we can keep on failing and dying until another sensible league comes along and decides to try it." He stared defiantly at the leader, feeling he had made up for his stupidity from earlier.

The man looked at him, his eyes cold as ice. "I see, and how do we know you will not turn on us if we let you in on our secrets?"

"Um…" Eli thought hard, but his thoughts had vanished into thin air.

"We kept her alive," Mia said, pointing at Silvia. Travis

moved behind Silvia and set his jaw.

"You seem to care about her a lot," the leader drawled, looking at Travis.

"Of course, I do, I—"

"We could not let her die," Eli cut in.

The man's eyes slid over to Eli's. "Boys always coo over her," he said simply.

Eli's face flushed. "I am not 'cooing' over her!" He turned to Travis and glared at him.

"Ah!" The leader had sniffed out what was really happening. "You. You fell for our lady here." The leader strode over to Travis and Silvia. Travis put an arm protectively over Silvia. "Ah. I see." The man smirked, but an angry gleam filled his eyes. "She betrayed us."

"She never did!" Travis intervened. "I can promise on my life that she never told me anything about your facilities or your plans. Just about herself and her parents." Travis's face turned scarlet. The man's gaze focused on Travis, scanning him for information.

"Sir," Mia said, stepping forward, "we need your help." She grimaced. "Our league can't take on League One by ourselves. We have proven that generation after generation. We need to team up. We need to stop this slaughtering of lives."

The man turned to study Mia. "And how will we

coordinate? We let you into our base; you will quickly overthrow us. You let us into your base. We overthrow you. It's instinct. No way around it."

"Yes, there is!" Eli insisted.

"You got this, man," Bryce muttered from behind him.

"Shut up," Eli hissed back.

"Sir. Mister…" Mia trailed off. Eli's eyes flickered to movement behind the leader.

Three other strangers were lurking in the doorway, standing behind the wall that separated the two sets of double doors.

He tried to warn Mia. "M—"

"We can figure this out," Mia continued.

"Mi—"

"Eli!" Mia snapped, turning sharply.

Just then, the three teenagers in the doorway jumped into the room and surrounded them. One smacked Bryce on the head with the butt of a knife, then grabbed Mia, one smacked Travis on the back of his head, then grabbed Harper, and another jumped on Eli. They left Layla, correctly identifying her as the weak link. The person who had smacked Travis then pulled Silvia aside, holding Harper's neck in a vice grip with one hand, and she gasped for air.

"Let go of me!" Silvia screamed. The boy looked at her, startled.

"Now, now," the leader of the league said placidly as if he saw attacks every day.

"S, you know who I am," the boy who had grabbed Harper said. Bryce groggily sat up and rubbed his head, dazed.

"No, I don't!" Silvia protested.

Mia struggled as her captor, a girl with long black hair, pulled her hair hard. She grunted, trying to punch the girl. Eli struggled under the weight of the person who had grabbed him.

"Did they corner you?" the girl who had Mia asked their leader. She had an interesting accent.

"Did they corner me? Let's see... Does it look like they cornered me?" the leader asked.

"Let me go!" Mia gasped. The girl slapped a dagger to her throat.

"Let her go!" Eli grunted from his spot on the floor. His attacker had his knee pressing painfully on his back.

"People, we are having a civilized meeting. Who cares if they are from League Four? They are no match for us," the opposing leader drawled.

On the floor, Travis moved slightly, groaning.

"S, are you okay?" the boy who had pulled Silvia aside

asked, concerned.

"Who are you?" Silvia asked.

"S, don't be stupid. Lockpicker." The girl who had a hold of Mia tossed him something shiny. The guy fiddled in front of Silvia, and then her hands were free. She stepped back from the strange boy. Travis groaned again and groggily sat up just in time to see the boy hug Silvia.

"Who are you?" she demanded, struggling.

"I missed you! Did they mistreat you?" the boy asked her, letting her go and stepping back.

Silvia backed up. "I don't know any of you," she insisted. His face fell.

"S— who?" Travis asked, slightly annoyed in his grogginess.

"Okay, you three," the leader announced. His league members looked at him. "Get behind me and drop your weapons."

"Sir—" the girl who had the knife to Mia's throat protested.

"Now."

The boy holding Eli reluctantly got up and stood behind his leader. The one who had hugged Silvia gazed at her as he backed up, but the girl holding Mia pressed the blade harder against Mia's throat.

"Is all this necessary?" the leader asked, looking at her. "What did I say?"

The girl's face turned to a sneer of regret. She shoved Mia away. Eli raced to catch her from falling to her knees. Mia pushed herself away from Eli and brushed her hair out of her face as the girl stalked behind her leader.

"Now," the leader said as silkily as ever.

Travis stumbled to his feet. Silvia, as if by instinct, moved to help steady him.

"Ouch," Travis groaned, reaching up to feel the back of his head.

"Now, are we going to be allies?" Layla piped up, folding her arms and glaring at each of the newcomers with distaste.

"L, lay off," Mia snapped at her. Layla stepped back, lowering her head. The boy who had hugged Silvia glared at Travis with distrust.

"Let me speak to your leader. We might come up with something. One of you will go get them," League Two's leader said.

"H," Mia said, still staring hard at him. "Go. Come back right outside this base."

Harper looked at Mia and massaged her neck from the aftermath of the boy's grip. "Okay," she said, unconvinced. "Hope to see you alive." She turned to exit the base.

Stiff silence weighed the air down. Travis and the boy who had knocked him out continued staring at each other. The boy's skin was white, and he had blond hair and blue eyes. The one who had tackled Eli had black hair, and his eyes were the same green shade as the girl who had attacked Mia.

"Who had this brilliant idea? Or possibly brilliant?" the leader asked.

"I did," Eli said stoutly. His hands tightened into a fist as he glared at the girl who had almost slit Mia's throat. "There is no other way to win." He looked at the leader and tried to look brave and buff like his brother instead of feeling like the tiniest piece of dust in the glare of a bright light.

The man's ears started smoking. "It's a new thought. But I have fought against you many times."

Eli stepped back. "You have?"

"You have?" the leader mimicked. "Yes, idiot."

Mia seemed to start in anger, despite calling Eli an idiot more times than she could have counted.

"We ran into each other as we attacked League One's base one day," the leader told them "I broke your leg and knocked you out. Your little girlfriend fended me off." He looked at Mia in sour disappointment.

"Oh, we're not together," Mia said. "No way."

Eli's heart turned to fire.

"She's pretty good at defending you," Layla said. Eli tried not to stomp his feet like a little kid.

They waited in silence. The three new strangers continued to study the four teenagers who studied them just as hard. After a long, silent wait, a commotion broke out outside.

"H is back," Mia said, refusing to turn her back on the new teens.

"B, go and escort our, er, guests inside," the leader commanded. The girl with black hair strode past him, making sure to smack her shoulder into Mia's shoulder as she stalked out the door. No one spoke, then the girl, B, led Gideon and Harper into the entrance.

"Well, well. We meet again," the leader said.

"Under unusual circumstances," Gideon said, surveying the League Two's leader with interest. "You lost some weight."

Mia sucked in a breath, and Eli figured that could not have been a good compliment.

"So, your league is sacrificing itself to help us?" League Two's leader asked, looking down on Gideon.

"No. We just want to get this job done. Get the brick and be free. One of my allies seems to have attached himself rather unfortunately to one of your allies, so... Why don't we try this together?" Gideon's tone was softer than usual. Not nearly as commanding. Could he be nervous?

"How can we meet so we will not get restless and attack each other?"

"When will we reveal our names and be one?" was Gideon's response.

The leader's lip curled up in disgust. "Sheldon," he said. "I'm Sheldon."

Chapter 7

Layla snorted. Harper slapped her hand over Layla's mouth.

"Good to meet you, um...ally, I suppose," Gideon said. "I'm—" He hesitated.

"You have to," Sheldon stated. "I told you mine. And your followers will have to introduce themselves too. I will make mine do the same. No worries."

"Worries right here," Bryce said as he shifted from foot to foot. Gideon turned to sMia and nodded. Mia swallowed. Eli had the unmistakable urge to grab Mia's hand but resisted.

"Mia," Mia said. Her eyes remained on B. B didn't blink.

"I'm Layla!" Layla piped up quickly.

They all turned to Bryce.

"Um... It's a nice day out," Bryce said, shifting awkwardly.

"B," Mia prompted.

"Bryce," he said with a huff.

"Travis."

"I'm Harper," Harper said. She didn't look happy to be announcing her name to strangers. The group from League

Four turned to face League Two's backups. The boy who had sized up Travis stepped forward.

Gideon cleared his throat. Eli could see the veins in Gideon's neck. "Gideon," he said, staring at Sheldon.

"I'm Wayne." The boy's voice was gruff.

"Brynlee," B said, her green eyes digging into Mia's with hate.

"I'm Joseph," Joseph said. He had the same accent as Brynlee. All the teens sized each other up; well, all but Silvia. Silvia shifted uncomfortably.

"Well, welcome to our...truce," Sheldon said uncomfortably.

Eli felt strange. He should have been happy that his idea was working, but it felt like something bad might happen soon.

"I have an idea about how we can show each other our bases," Gideon said.

"And?" Sheldon drawled.

"We should split our teams up. Some from my team will get a tour of your facilities, and some from your league will go with some from my team. Each person who does not go into their base doesn't carry defensive weapons," Gideon proposed to Sheldon, daring him to contradict him.

Sheldon turned to study the three teenagers. They straightened up even more. "Wayne and Joseph, you go with them. Brynlee, I trust you can handle their team in our base?"

"Of course, I can," Brynlee said, fiddling with the handle of her dagger.

"Mia, Eli, you go with her," Gideon said.

"Silvia, c'mon. Let's get you settled in again." Wayne stepped forward and grabbed her hand. Travis bristled and stepped forward as well.

"She is not going anywhere with you," Travis said.

Wayne glared at Travis. "Why? Why should she trust you? You kidnapped her."

"Because we-we—" Travis stopped himself.

"What?" Wayne stiffened. "Is that why you—" He cut himself off.

Travis grabbed Silvia's other hand.

"I see," Wayne said sulkily.

Silvia looked from guy to guy, obviously uncomfortable. "I don't know either of you that well."

"Wayne, go. Now. They are showing you their base. As for you, I do not trust you in my base," Sheldon said to Gideon.

Gideon glared at Sheldon. "And I do not trust you in mine."

"We will stay here," Sheldon offered. With that agreement, both leaders grinned at each other unnervingly.

"Well, c'mon," Brynlee said. "Let's get this over with." She stalked through the second set of doors that led into the base. With one last look at Gideon, Eli and Mia followed. Mia strode ahead of him, radiating confidence.

~

League Two's base was hauntingly familiar. Same layout, same hallways. There were a few different rooms, however. One stopped Mia in her tracks with a gasp. It was a large gym, with a running track in the center.

"Now that's better than the treadmills we have!" she said, pointing, clearly forgetting her disgruntled feelings towards Brynlee.

She took a hesitant step towards Brynlee. "May—" She broke off, her face flooded with embarrassment.

"Sure. Go ahead," Brynlee grumbled.

Mia became a blur. She was on that track in a split second. Brynlee and Eli stood next to each other, stiffness emanating between them.

"So, how long have you been here?" he asked. She looked at him as if he was the stupidest person that she had ever met. He probably was.

"Um...my whole life. Probably the same as you, I'm guessing. However, we are not here to get to know each other. We are here to be done with this masquerade." She folded her arms and looked away. Mia sprinted up to them; her cheeks were flushed, and her smile lit up her whole face. Eli's insides fluttered.

"Nice track!" Mia said, barely panting. She had gone around it about five times in less than five seconds.

"Are we ready to go on, then?" Brynlee asked.

"Yeah," Mia said, her face falling at Brynlee's coldness towards them. They walked on.

"So, you just *came across* Silvia, did you?" Brynlee asked Eli.

"Uh…yeah," Eli said. "That's pretty much what happened."

"Uh huh. And you did not bother to find out where she was from?"

"She didn't know who she was," Eli protested.

"Really, that's a good joke."

Eli's fists clenched. "Why does everyone think that we are pretending about these things? It's not a joke!" Eli gritted out, facing Brynlee.

"Uh huh," she said, obviously unconvinced. "You know, that's cruel. To take someone's teammate and then turn her against her friends."

"We did not take her on purpose!" Eli shot back, outraged.

"Well, that's your plan, isn't it? Get on Sheldon's nice side, then stab him in the back!"

"That's not our plan!" Eli insisted. The two were nose-to-nose.

Mia intervened, pushing both of them away. "Enough! We are here for the tour. Are we done yet?"

Brynlee glared at Eli, who wondered why girls had to be so mad at him all the time. Why couldn't any of them be on his side? Well, other than Addy. She was a different story.

"We are just about done," Brynlee huffed. "Just one more spot to show you."

When they made it back to the entranceway, the others had just materialized outside League Two's building. The three were surprised to see Gideon and Sheldon talking and laughing like old friends.

"What's this?" Brylee asked sharply as she and the others entered.

Gideon immediately stopped laughing and snapped to attention. "Nothing important." His lips twitched as if he were fighting back a laugh.

The others walked into the entrance room and resumed their places from earlier.

"So. We must have a meeting with our leagues," Sheldon said, looking more relaxed than he had before.

"I will look around and send someone to get back to you,"

Gideon said. He turned to leave, bending down to pick up his league's weapons on the way out. He tossed everyone their weapons. Silvia looked back at the people from her league.

"Silvia, where are you going?" Wayne asked.

"Home," she said. Travis's chest just about popped as he swelled with pride.

"That is not your home!" Wayne lunged towards her, but Brynlee held him back, glaring daggers at Eli.

"I don't know any of you," Silvia said simply. She turned and left with the others.

~

Eli opened his eyes and blinked them in the bright fluorescent light of Gideon's "chamber."

"Well, that went well." Harper's voice broke the slightly stunned silence.

"I'm rather surprised," Gideon said. He seemed more relaxed after his encounter with Sheldon.

"I should not have gone." Everyone turned to stare at Silvia.

"What?" Harper asked.

"Why? You helped us so much," Travis said.

"Now I'm even more confused," she confessed. "It seems like strangers care about me... But I have gotten to know some of you slightly, and I feel almost like I have known you my whole life."

"Silvia." Travis stepped forward and grabbed her hand. "We will do our best to help you."

Gideon turned away, disgusted at this sappiness.

Silvia looked down. "I honestly don't know who that boy was…um…Wayne."

"I know, you forgot," Travis said. Mia turned to leave and started down the hall, but Eli had a thought.

"Hey!" He hurried after Mia. "Hey, Mia," he said, catching up to her and panting slightly, to his embarrassment.

"What?" she asked, an edge to her voice.

"I'm sorry for being such an idiot back there," he said, stumbling to keep up with her fast pace.

She stopped and turned to face him. "I don't blame you… Not one hundred percent anyways. All those people."

Eli stepped slightly closer to her as his heart raced. "It's just that… I don't know." He looked down at his feet. He could just see the tips of her fingers in his peripheral vision.

"Hey," Mia said as tears burned the corners of his eyes. "You are not the Eli I knew." She paused, and he looked up into her coffee eyes. She smiled at him. "I rather like this new Eli."

He awkwardly reached out his hand and took hers. Her expression changed immediately. She snapped her hand out of his as the lunch bell rang.

"Or maybe I don't." She stormed away, leaving him looking after her in bewilderment.

"Nice try."

Eli jumped, kinking his neck in the process. He painfully looked around to see Bryce and Harper. Harper looked slightly amused. Eli felt his cheeks heat up.

Eli shifted, averting his eyes from Harper and Bryce. "It's lunchtime, right? I'm assuming that's what the bell meant."

"Yeah," Harper said. "C'mon, let's eat!"

Chapter 8

Mia avoided Eli during lunch that day. He was not surprised. She almost always avoided him now. Right when Eli was going to get up to put his plate away, Gideon stood up and got everyone's attention.

"I have an announcement!" he bellowed. The room grew quiet. "We have an alliance with League Two!"

The room filled with gasps and mutters.

"That's foolishness!" someone called out.

"It's a risk, yes. But necessary. If anyone knows of a place where two groups can meet together safely, let me know. We are not going to let the whole league into our base. This also means no more killing anyone from League Two. They are our allies now."

More grumbles filled the room.

"Until they stab us in the back," someone said. "We should just give up now!"

"You are all dismissed!" Gideon interjected.

"Come on," Bryce said, walking up to Eli. "Let's go see if we can find a meeting spot with Harper."

"Alone? Outside?" Eli wondered. "You know, I have not had very good experiences outside."

"We got this!" Harper said, bounding up to Bryce and Eli.

"Okay," Eli said, doubt in his voice.

~

The three walked along the sidewalk, light glinting off their suits. The concrete sidewalks melted into brick buildings, and roads intersect each other here and there. "It's a beautiful day!" Harper sighed, inhaling the warm air.

"It is," Eli agreed. He was just about to ask Harper something when the strangest sound he had ever heard split through the silent day.

"Roof!"

"What was that?" Eli asked, snapping to attention.

"Roof! Roof!"

The sound came closer, along with the sound of something skittering along a sidewalk. The three backed into a defensive position, backs to each other, turning in a circle. There was silence, just a snuffling sound, then out from an alley burst a medium-sized creature that had four legs, a tail sort of like Gideon's when he transformed, and a long snout. It shook its tail energetically and bounded up to the three teenagers.

Eli started, forgetting to stay in a defensive position. "What?"

"Roof!" the creature exclaimed, jumping up and spreading its wet tongue over his face.

"Ugh!" Eli stumbled back.

"Roof *roof!*"

Bryce and Harper stared at it in shock.

"What is it?" Harper asked, crouching so that she was at eye level with it.

It bounded over to her and slid its tongue over her hand. "Ah!" She stumbled back.

"Roof roof!"

It continued to…celebrate? Eli was not sure. He straightened his shirt and walked over to it.

"It doesn't seem dangerous," he commented. The thing trotted over to him and wriggled its body, looking at him happily. Its fur was mostly black and medium-long, and it had pointy ears and black eyes.

It pranced over to Bryce, who recoiled. "Looks vicious."

"Whmmm," the creature said. It looked hurt.

"You hurt its feelings, Bryce!" Eli reproved, noticing it tuck its tail between its hind legs.

"It's okay, I think," Harper said, walking over to it and tentatively patting its back.

The thing quickly acted happy again.

"Roof roof!" It exclaimed as it trotted in the direction it had come.

"No! Don't go!" Harper called after it.

It looked back and exclaimed, "Roof!" It wandered again, stopped, looked back, and repeated, "Roof!"

"I think it wants us to follow it," Eli said, staring curiously at the strange thing. It shook its tail and bounded out of sight.

"Wait!" Harper shouted.

"Harper!" Bryce called to her, who had run after it. Eli followed close behind her.

"Oh, great," Bryce moaned, then ran after the other two. The hairy creature led them down several alleys to the tall, brick wall surrounding all four leagues. It seemed to go up forever, disappearing into white fluffy things.

"Roof!" it exalted when Harper and Eli caught up to it. It bounded to the wall and disappeared.

"Where?" Harper looked around.

"Roof!"

"I can hear it! But where did it go?" Bryce trotted up, his hand clutching his side.

"That's what I was—" Harper started to say, but Eli interrupted.

"Guys. You're gonna want to see this." His voice filled with wonder.

"What?"

"Roof! Roof!" the creature's cheerful voice sang from somewhere. Harper and Bryce crouched down to look and gasped.

There, in the middle of the unbreakable wall, was a hole. It was about four feet wide and two feet tall. Its jagged edges showed it had not been carefully cut into, but that was not the incredible part. The incredible part lay beyond.

Through the hole, Eli could see the red brick of buildings. There were sidewalks surrounding them, and the light beat down so bright that he had to squint. The part of the ground that was not covered with the sidewalk was covered in some sort of green, natural material. The creature was bouncing around, making noises in the green stuff. It chased something that was bright pink and orange that fluttered in the air. Rough-looking brown things went from the green up and out of sight, shadows underneath them.

"Roof! Roof!"

A soft thing caressed Eli's face as he looked through, making him jump. "What was that?" He looked around, but everything was normal.

"Is that… Is that what it's like outside of this?" Harper's voice choked up.

Lining the sidewalks were thicker green with rainbow shapes atop them. The creature ran over to one of the colorful objects and sniffed it. Then it noticed the others looking through the hole.

"Roof! Roof!" It bounded over to the hole and squeezed through it partway, and slobbered on Eli.

"Ugh!"

It backed up again and made a circle as if saying, *C'mon! The world awaits you to explore with me!*

"I don't believe it." Bryce's voice filled with a strange tone. Eli slid back and sat on his heels, staring at his friends. They sat up.

"What is that?" Eli asked.

"It's—it's the real world," Harper said, her eyes brimming with tears. "I never thought I would be able to see it." The warm thing caressed their legs, and all three leaped back like it was acid.

"What was that?" Bryce yelled.

"I don't know," Eli said, starting to shake. "We should go."

"But—" Harper looked longingly at the hole that they could just squeeze through.

"Harper, we can't leave the others," Eli insisted. "Let's go. Maybe we shouldn't tell anyone about this."

"But-"

"It's too… I don't know," Eli said. His mind filled with the image he had seen of the creature prancing around as if it was dancing in the bright light.

"Roof! Roof!"

They turned reluctantly and started walking away.

"We'll get there someday," Eli said, putting a hand on Harper's shoulder. She looked at him sadly.

"I hope so," she whispered.

"Do you think that people live out there?" Eli asked, skeptical that there could be life outside of this prison.

"Yeah," Harper said. "The world can't be all about war, can it? Get down!" She pulled the two boys to the ground as several bullets whizzed by their heads. They lay on the ground, peering up to see what had happened. Eli's ears picked up only the sound of the trio's fast breaths of fright.

"What was that?" Bryce whispered.

"Shh!" Harper hissed. They stayed on the ground. Then, three figures appeared from around the corner, all wearing black sweatshirts with hoods pulled up. The one in the middle stopped and stepped back.

"Oh." The voice sounded familiar. "Never mind, guys, let's go."

It was Brynlee's voice. She pulled her hood back and looked down at the three.

Harper was first to her feet. "Brynlee!"

Bryce and Eli scrambled up next. Eli looked curiously at the other shadowed faces. Brynlee ignored Harper.

"Brynlee," she repeated as Brynlee stepped to leave. She hesitated and turned stiffly to them.

"What are you doing here?" Bryce asked. "And why did you try to kill us?"

"Bryce!" Harper snapped.

The other two pulled their hoods down, revealing the faces of Wayne and Joseph.

"Why does it matter?" Brynlee asked. She had the same calm voice as her leader.

"Why did you shoot at us?" Bryce asked gruffly.

"Why do you ask so many questions?" Wayne retorted.

"It doesn't matter!" Brynlee raised her voice.

Eli suddenly got a vision of Mia standing there, screaming the same thing. He blinked the image away.

"Let's go," Brynlee said, sounding bored and annoyed.

"What are you doing anyway?" Bryce asked. Harper rolled her eyes.

"Looking for a place to meet," Joseph said. Everyone looked at him. He was the silent and stern-looking type.

"So are we!" Eli said.

Brynlee looked like she could have disintegrated the three people standing before her just by staring at them. "How special," she said, her tone dripping with sarcasm. "Now can we go?"

Harper opened her mouth to respond when a building exploded right behind Brynlee, Wayne, and Joseph. Their bodies flew forward from the force of the explosion, landing in a heap by Eli's feet. Immediately, the air filled with smoke, gunfire, and shouts. The six frenemies scrambled backward, trying to get out of harm's way.

"Oh gosh," Harper gasped, tugging Brynlee's stunned body farther back with her.

Eli and Bryce did the same to Wayne and Joseph.

A group of people in black suits with three red lines on the shoulder came pouring from the direction of the building. They didn't notice the teenagers on the ground. Instead, they shot their guns at people wearing gold suits, who were backing up and returning fire.

"League Three is attacking League— League—" Harper could not finish.

"Move, move!" Eli hissed to the others.

"To the hole!" Harper insisted.

"No!" Eli retaliated.

"What?" Brynlee stirred and looked up groggily. She had a nasty, bloody spot on her head, and her face had turned a pasty green.

"We need to move before they see us! *Go!*" Eli urged.

They continued scuffling along the alley as the suited troops advanced on each other. Suddenly, one of the people from League Three jerked and looked straight at them. They all froze.

"Oh, Mia, we need you!" Harper groaned. Eli silently agreed.

The figure turned and started walking like a robot, heedless of the shouts and bullets flying around it. Like many in League Three, the figure had a black helmet on, making it impossible to see their face.

"Let's go!" Bryce said, standing up and turning, only to face a dead end. They had cornered themselves in an alley that was cut off by the wall. Eli and Harper stepped in front of the dazed bodies. Brynlee grabbed Eli's and Harper's legs and hoisted herself up, groaning a sickly groan and stumbling back into Bryce.

"Stay down," Harper ordered.

"N-no," Brynlee insisted, drawing her dagger, but

slumping to the ground in dizziness.

The figure, a woman, judging by her outline and slim waist, continued to approach them.

"What do you want?" Eli asked, jerking his chin up and stepping slightly in front of Harper.

"Die," the voice said. "Die, die, die."

"We are not in the battle," Bryce said unhelpfully from behind Eli and Harper.

"You shut up," Harper said.

"Let me h-help," Brynlee tried again. She stood up and, this time, fell onto Eli.

Eli fell forward and landed with his hands in front of him. His chin smacked the pavement. He painfully raised his chin and blinked hard.

"Go, Eli!" Harper urged. "Use your flying power. I know you still have it in you. I'll— I'll fend her off!"

"But-"

"Eli!" Harper screamed at him.

The woman stopped and pointed her gun right at Eli's head.

"Fly?" he asked. Just then, he felt his body jerk. He looked down to see that he was hovering inches from the ground. "Ah!"

"Yes, Eli!" Harper shouted in delight. "Go get Gideon!"

119

Eli's thoughts blurred. He looked at the woman, and suddenly, he propelled forward and slightly upright as the woman fired her gun. The pavement cracked right at the spot that Eli had just been in. He soared above the woman and tried to think what to do. He could not seem to control where he was going.

"Watch out, Eli!" He looked down at Harper's frightened cry.

The woman was still training her gun on him. Without thinking, he plummeted for her. He smacked her head, and she fell to the side. Her helmet cracked as she hit the pavement, and rolled away. The gun had fallen out of her hand and skittered away to Harper's feet. Eli landed, turned, and gasped. The woman had long, wavy brown hair. She blinked dazedly, revealing brown eyes.

"No." He stumbled backwards and tripped over Wayne's body. Wayne stirred and moaned.

"Eli," Harper breathed.

The woman pushed herself up and looked right at Eli.

"Mom?" Eli breathed.

Chapter 9

B ut, but—" Bryce stood there, dumbfounded. Brynlee struggled, trying to get up, but she kept falling back.

"Stay down!" Harper finally snapped at Brynlee.

"She - she - there were eyewitnesses that she was shot!" Bryce gasped out.

Eli's mom stared at Eli. The only reason he recognized her was the photo of him with his dad and Gideon. Eli's mom shook her head and got unsteadily to her feet. She blinked and swayed back and forth.

"Um… MaKenzee?" Harper asked, tentatively stepping forward.

The woman's eyes snapped to Harper. "What?" she asked.

"Yes!" A triumphant cry came from behind Harper. Brynlee, still dumb from her fall, had lunged forward and grabbed the gun at Harper's feet. She aimed it shakily at MaKenzee.

"No!" Harper cried.

Brynlee's firm face said that she did not care what was happening. Harper's cry alerted a few stragglers to their presence, and three people from League Three broke ranks and ran down the alley.

"M! Get out of here! Finish them and go!" a voice called.

MaKenzee turned unsteadily toward the voice, just as the blast from the gun that Brynlee was holding echoed around the alley. MaKenzee screamed in pain and crumpled to the sidewalk. The three people who had been approaching her halted.

"B!" Harper angrily yelled at Brynlee. "She is on our side! But we need to leave! Eli— no—get to the group! Bryce, take them all to our base! I'll get MaKenzee!"

"But-" Bryce tried to change her mind.

"Eli doesn't remember how! Go!"

The three strangers had reloaded their guns during Harper's orders and looked prepared to fire.

"But—" Eli started to protest, but Harper's glare advised him otherwise. He dove for the pile and grabbed Brynlee's wrist, seizing a fistful of Wayne's hair as Bryce reached down for Joseph and Wayne. They closed their eyes.

~

Eli opened his eyes. They had appeared in a heap in the middle of their entranceway, right in front of them Gideon and Norah who split apart in surprise.

"What's this?" Gideon snapped.

Eli looked up and got to his feet.

"What happened?" Gideon asked again as Bryce stood up, and Joseph and Wayne twitched. Brynlee stood up and wobbled like she was drunk.

"Let me—!" she started, but her voice dropped.

"What?" Norah looked to Gideon.

"We kind of had an incident," Eli said. His mind was spinning, the hole in the wall, the strange creature, his mom... His mom. She wasn't dead.

"Tell me," Gideon commanded.

"I think we need to get these guys to the sick ward first."

"Ew!" Bryce cried. Brynlee had just lost her lunch on the floor.

"I agree," Gideon said, averting his eyes with disgust. He spoke into a walkie. "We need five medics to come to the entrance immediately. We have some...injured allies." They helped Brynlee out of the entranceway and went back to drag Wayne and Joseph out. Joseph blinked his eyes open as the door swung shut behind them.

"What happened?" he croaked out.

"Later," Eli muttered.

The medics arrived. They halted when they saw the people from a different league but carted them off at Gideon's instructions. It took two medics to drag Brynlee, who seemed convinced that they were still in danger.

"Now," Gideon said, turning toward Eli and Bryce. "What happened?"

Before either could explain, Harper appeared right in front of them with a half-limp MaKenzee trying to resist. A nasty bloody wound gaped open on her left arm.

Gideon gasped, and Norah passed out right on the spot.

"Norah!"

He bent down and shook her. She woke up with a gasp.

"I need another medic!" Gideon roared into the walkie. He stood up and blinked in bewilderment at MaKenzee.

"Where did you find her?" he asked sharply. Then, his eyes—could it be? His eyes filled with tears. He angrily brushed them away and approached her. He put a firm hand on her shoulder, and she stopped resisting to look up at him.

"Mom?" he asked.

"What? Let me go!" the woman cried out.

Another medic clattered up to them and stopped in shock as he spotted MaKenzee. "MaKenzee?"

Just then, her pain must have caught up with her. She gasped and collapsed on the floor, clutching her bullet wound.

"I'll take care of her," the doctor said. He spoke into his

walkie, and more people rushed over to help take MaKenzee and norah away.

Gideon's face paled. "Really, what happened?"

With many unhelpful interruptions from Bryce, they told their story. Eli made sure that they skipped the part about the strange thing and the hole.

"And we managed to transport here," Eli finished.

"But I don't know... Why didn't she... Mom's alive?" Gideon turned to Eli, seeming to have forgotten that the others were there. "There were eyewitnesses of her death." Gideon put his hands to his hair. "And how would she not recognize us?"

Eli and Harper looked at each other and realized the same thing and shouted simultaneously, for once startling Gideon.

"The bullet!"

They looked at each other and grinned.

"It all makes sense!" Eli said.

Harper nodded. "We thought she had been killed, but really they had just shot her with a bullet like they used to shoot Eli and Silvia!"

"And when she blacked out, they thought she was dead because they were too busy trying to fight for their lives," Eli added. "And the other league caught her, and she woke up in their base, and they trained her against us!" A sick feeling filled his stomach as he realized that was pretty much what they had done to Silvia. He shook off the thought. *We were trying to help her. We did not really kidnap her, did we?*

"I don't..." Gideon's voice trailed off. Eli had never, in his memory, seen Gideon so speechless. "Mom," he said simply.

Eli got a thrilling realization. "Then Dad might not be dead either!"

Gideon looked at Eli. "I don't know about that. But I need to think. Everyone, go away, don't go out again today."

"But aren't you worried that League Three will get the brick before us?" Harper asked, a worried crease on her forehead.

"No. Kayla and her second group are going on a raid now. With luck, we will have a lead soon."

Harper looked slightly disappointed. "Okay. Come on, guys. Let's find Mia and Travis. They will want to hear this!"

~

"You mean...your mom?" Mia's voice squeaked as she looked at Eli with tears in her eyes. He and Harper had just finished telling Travis, Silvia, and Mia what had happened, almost all of it anyway. "That means your dad could be alive, too!"

"Not to mention your parents," Eli said and immediately regretted it.

Her sympathetic look turned sour. "I don't think so." She looked away.

All this time, Silvia had been staring off into space; finally, Travis took her hand, and she looked around. "What?" she asked.

"Are you thinking of your parents?" he asked her.

"Yes," she whispered. "The people I did not know said that I was their daughter. But I don't remember, so I don't know."

"You showed me a picture of them," Travis said. "From before. And those are your parents. I am selfish in keeping you here. We should take you back." He started standing up.

"No," Silvia said. They all looked at her. "No." Travis sat down. "I don't know that place. I like it here."

Travis grinned at her.

"We should go check on Brynlee and the others," Harper suggested.

Mia's face turned stony. "I'm good."

The group got up to depart. Mia started walking away, but Eli hurried to catch up with her and touched her shoulder, trying to avoid the dagger eyes he'd receive for holding her hand again.

"What?" she asked. She seemed emotional for some reason.

"We will find them. I promise. I will do my best. Your parents. It will be okay."

She stared into his eyes for a moment, and Eli got a strange urge to step forward and -

But she turned and stalked away.

"It's never gonna happen, buddy."

Eli turned to see Bryce standing behind him. "Why do you always have to be here when I talk to Mia?"

Bryce just shrugged, turned, and left.

"Let's go," Eli said to Harper.

~

Harper and Eli looked into the long room lined with beds covered in white sheets as medics hurried this way and that. There were at least half a dozen people in the bay, not counting the five new people. Norah was sitting up in bed now, shakily sipping a cup of water.

The two walked over to where Brynlee, Wayne, and Joseph were stationed. Joseph and Brynlee were awake. Joseph looked at the ceiling while Brynlee was sitting on the edge of the bed. She obviously wanted to get up and leave, but nurses kept on shooting her disapproving glances. She glanced up when she saw Harper and Eli walking toward her. They pulled up chairs and sat by her.

"How are you?" Harper asked quietly. Brynlee remained sullen.

"Hey—it's not our fault that you and the others were knocked out! We didn't know that an attack was coming," Eli defended himself and Harper.

Brynlee looked at him and gave an exaggerated eye roll. "Yeah. Well, if your *friend* did not stall us, we would have been on our way." She flinched the slightest bit. It was obvious she was in pain, but she refused to show it.

"Bryce will be Bryce." Harper sighed. "But in all honesty, you did try to kill us."

Brynlee looked down. "We thought you were the enemy spying on us."

Harper and Eli looked around. Joseph had propped himself up slightly and looked over at Wayne's bed.

"A day ago, we would have been," Harper said. "But not anymore."

"Anyways, I'm tired." Brynlee lay back down on her bed.

She's lying, Joseph mouthed to Harper and Eli. They got up to leave. As they passed his bed, Joseph stopped them. "Hey, she's cool. She's just wounded about Sheldon making her let Mia go... Brynlee doesn't like to show mercy. I'd know. Brynlee's my sister." Joseph grimaced.

"That's good to know," Harper said and steered Eli out of the room. As the door swung shut behind them, she leaned over to whisper to Eli, "We better tell Mia to watch her back, just in case."

Eli nodded. His stomach jumped at the sound of Mia's

name. Suddenly, he halted, remembering his mom. He turned and looked through the door's window. He scanned the beds and spotted one that was covered from view by a bunch of white curtains. Many medics were going in and out with tools.

Eli felt a hand on his shoulder. He looked to see Harper staring at the bed as well. "Let's go. She'll be okay."

Chapter 10

Bryce caught up with Eli and Harper as they aimlessly wandered around, not knowing what else to do. They were just approaching the entranceway when a wild and disheveled Kayla stumbled through the door.

"What happened?" Harper asked, rushing over to steady her and help her through the second doorway.

Kayla just shook her head. She pulled two energy drinks seemingly out of nowhere that she handed to Eli and Bryce, then she thrust a frappuccino into Harper's hands.

"The others, where are they?" Harper asked.

Kayla just shook her head and sat on the ground. She put her face in her hands. Her pink hair drooped over her face as her shoulders shook.

"Kayla, what is it?" Harper prompted. "Where are Addy and Layla? And did Wade go with you?"

She nodded.

"What? Bryce, get Gideon," Harper said.

Kayla shook her head frantically, looking up. Her eyes were red, and tears streamed down her face. "Don't, he'll be furious," she choked out. But Bryce had already run off.

"What happened? Where are the others?" Harper repeated.

"Gideon will want to know the same. Let's only make her recount her story once," Eli said, for once reading a girl's emotions correctly.

Harper looked at him in surprise but nodded. "Come on, let's get her out of the doorway."

Eli moved to Kayla's other side, and they carried her to a nook next to the entranceway. Bryce and Gideon appeared on the far end of the hall and swiftly walked over.

"What is it? Where are the others? What happened, Kayla?" Gideon asked.

Kayla looked down as she took a shaky breath. "They…they…"

"Got kidnapped?" Bryce interrupted. Harper glared at him from where she sat on the couch, trying to comfort Kayla. "No big deal. We'll just send Brynlee in after them."

"Shut up," Harper snapped.

"They did not make it out," she managed, wiping away tears.

"Well, we will just send in another raid to go get them." Gideon turned on his heels.

"No! Gideon." Everyone turned to her. "They - they died."

"All of them? Wade, Layla, and Addy?" Harper asked,

aghast.

Kayla nodded as tears continued to fall into her lap.

"What is the story behind this?" Gideon asked, sitting in a chair and staring at her hard. Eli felt that his brother should at least have some sympathy. When Kayla had said that they all had died, it had felt like a hot iron had gone through his body.

"We had made it into the entranceway," Kayla started.

"No way!" Bryce said, earning himself another glare from Harper. She had mastered that move well.

"League One was distracted by a battle from League Three. We made it in not seven feet when some members of League One spotted us. They had guns with them. They immediately started charging and calling for reinforcement. I tried to make them drowsy, but it worked too well. Addy did something with her eyes that made one of the guards crumple to the floor steaming, and Wade got his boomerang out and was going to throw it when he and Layla were blasted with my drowsiness." She paused and handed Gideon a Gatorade. "Layla had just gone into one of her annoying speeches, trying to distract the guards when two guards fired from behind us. One bullet went right through Wade, and he collapsed." She gasped for air. "Then…then, Addy and Layla started slowing down. Addy fell asleep on the spot and fell to the floor. I was too busy trying to get around the other guards to notice. When another shot came, I looked back just in time to see Layla jumping in front of the bullet to spare Addy. It hit her in the head." She stopped to wipe

133

more tears from her eyes.

"Then I don't get it. Addy didn't die," Gideon said.

"I'm getting there," Kayla snapped. "I stopped when I saw both Wade's and Layla's bodies on the ground. One of the sluggish guards slapped me aside with his gun. He aimed it at Addy, who was asleep on the floor and blasted her five times. I don't even remember how I got out of there; all I remember is opening my eyes and finding myself in the entranceway." She slumped on the couch and buried her face again.

Gideon looked grim.

"But how do you know that they're not just going to wake up without their memories?" Eli asked, feeling hot anger inside for the enemy who had ended the lives of people on his team.

"I just know. When Mia told me the story about you getting shot, you were only out for a few seconds. Wade had been out for at least a minute, and he did not move an inch." She stopped talking and refused to answer any more questions.

"Well, at least we've got one problem solved," Gideon said. Everyone but Kayla stared at him. "Silvia will move in with you. Bryce, no - Eli, go and tell Silvia that. Last I saw, she and Travis were in the workout room."

"Um... Tell them that three people died, so Silvia is going to move in with Kayla?"

"Go," Gideon said. His face looked slightly pained.

Eli got up and left, his face burning with anger at what had happened. Sure, he did not know Layla that well. The only times he could remember being around her, she had been annoying. And Addy, he did not know her well either, but she was the only girl he had ever gone on a date with. Still, the loss hit him like a truck. He felt like a zombie walking down all the long, metal corridors with blank walls. He heard the creature's "roofs" again in his head and saw the brightness outside. He remembered that strange smell and the green ground.

~

Eli walked into the workout room to find Silvia doing sit-ups and Travis holding her feet. They both looked at him and stopped what they were doing when he walked into the room.

"What is it?" Travis asked. His eyes were studying Eli's pale and angry face.

"Um...I don't know how to break this to you..." Eli stopped, and Travis helped Silvia to her feet. "Silvia. You are going to be Kayla's roommate."

"But Layla is her roommate."

Eli looked down. "Not anymore."

"What?" Travis asked.

"Um... She, Wade, and Addy died."

"What!" Travis yelled.

"In the raid on Base One. Kayla was the only one who

survived." Eli felt the words coming out of his mouth, but they barely even sounded like words to him. He felt far away.

"You're pranking me."

Eli's blood pressure rose. "Why does everyone think I'm pranking them?" He put his fists on his hips. "Why would I prank about something like that, Travis?" His eyes filled with angry tears.

"Let's go, Travis," Silvia said, slipping her hand into Travis'. Eli's heart filled with strange, hot jealousy to see Travis holding a girl's hand. "So I can get moved in."

As she led Travis past him, Travis stopped. "I'm sorry," he said.

Eli looked straight ahead, eyes still stinging. He jerked his head up in acknowledgment. The two left, leaving him in silence. Fury billowed up inside him, and he had to get it out. He got on a treadmill and tried to run his anger out, but that failed. He started doing push-ups when Mia walked into the room and halted when she saw him. He continued exercising. A single tear had slid down his face.

Mia walked over and looked down at him. "Eli."

He ignored her. His arms were burning, but that did not stop him. The pain was nothing compared to the confusion of the past twenty-four hours of his life.

"Eli," she repeated.

He stopped, panting. He got to his feet.

"I heard what happened today with Kayla... I'm sorry," she said, looking down.

Eli was stunned. Before he could say anything, she stepped forward and hugged him. Sure, it was quick, and she was out of there as fast as she could, but it was still a hug. He stood there, dazed. All the fury and hurt had left him with that simple embrace. He left the room and went to his bunk, where he found Bryce lying on his bed. Eli climbed up into his bunk.

"Hey," he said.

"Hey," Bryce grunted. He held a book in his hands, glancing up from the pages. "You okay, dude? Your face looks weird."

Such a Bryce thing to say, Eli thought through the numbness in his mind.

"Uh...I guess," was all he could muster. *What goes on inside girls' minds?*

~

At dinner that night, Mia sat at his table beside Travis, next to Silvia. Their table was unusually empty without the presence of Layla and Addy. Kayla had joined them, though she did not eat much. She had a small spoonful of mashed potatoes on her plate. She touched nothing. Eli's eyes kept on drooping.

"Oh. Sorry," Kayla said as Eli just kept himself from face-planting into his spaghetti. She handed him a tall bottle of Mountain Dew.

"How do you...?" he started to ask, but she interrupted him.

"It's part of my blessing. If you can call it that. I have a never-ending supply of energy drinks." She handed Silvia a fufu drink.

"Thanks," Silvia slurred out.

"I'm no fighter," Kayla said glumly, staring at her plate with distaste. "I should just go to bed."

"And miss the meeting? Gideon would be furious," Mia said.

"Hey, it was not your fault that they died. You were distracted," Eli butted in.

"Oh, really?" Kayla asked. "I was distracted? Yeah, just the point. I could not protect them." Kayla got up and left, Eli watched her leave.

Mia yelped. Eli turned and saw a dagger at Mia's throat.

Chapter 11

Eli's gaze flit behind Mia to see Brynlee standing behind her, dagger in hand. Joseph and a groggy-looking Wayne stood awkwardly behind her.

"Don't think it's over," Brynlee growled.

"Bryn, really?" Joseph asked. Both he and Wayne held trays of food.

Brynlee rolled her eyes and removed the dagger. "Can't I have some fun? I had to let her go. You know how I feel about that."

"Just stop," Joseph said. His eyes flitted to Harper, then back to his sister.

"Bu—" Brynlee started to protest, but her voice cut off; however, her mouth kept on moving as if she was talking.

"Wha...?" Eli's eyes slid to Wayne, whose gaze landed on Brynlee, concentrating hard. When he looked away, Brynlee grumbled something and went over to them.

"Sorry about her. She hates loose cannons." Joseph apologized.

"Loose cannons?" Mia asked.

"Sheldon made her let you go," Joseph said, sliding uninvited into a vacant seat. Wayne and Brynlee followed suit.

"So... I'm guessing you are going to come to our meeting tonight?" Eli asked them stiffly.

"Gideon says we must," Brynlee said as she grabbed a plate off of Joseph's tray.

"Hey, can you show me how to do that shutting up thing?" Harper asked Wayne.

Wayne looked at her in surprise.

"There are times I would like to shut Bryce up," Harper said.

"Hey!" Bryce protested.

"He can't teach it; it's his blessing," Brynlee answered for him. When she looked down to cut into her meat, Joseph mouthed in a sassy way, *It's his blessing.* Eli expected to hear a snort of laughter coming from Layla, but of course, nothing came.

"So, how long are you planning on pigging out in our base?" Mia asked.

"Mia," Harper snapped at her.

Brynlee put her fork down and glared at Mia. "As long as your so-called leader Gideon tells us to." She leaned towards Mia, fists clenching. "He may be a leader, but he's a weak one."

Mia stood up, her hand flying to her belt where she kept her black weapon, which Eli had still not gotten a close look at. Brynlee drew her dagger and held it threateningly before her. Both girls were nose-to-nose, ready for combat.

"Okay. Let's cool it over here," Harper said. She waved her hands, making some sparkly white stuff, and a cold gust blew at Brynlee and Mia, which forced them back into their chairs. Eli gaped.

"My blessing," she said, smiling at him. "I can make sleet come out of my hands."

"Sleet?" Eli asked. Harper shrugged.

Brynlee rubbed her hands up and down her arms, looking almost admiringly at Harper. "Not a bad blessing."

"What's yours? As you seem to have none," Mia said. Harper slapped her hand over Mia's mouth.

"To hold a grudge," Brynlee said.

"Yeah, right," Wayne snorted. Brynlee looked back at her plate and finished eating in stony silence.

~

There were three extra chairs at the meeting that night. People were giving the three people from League Two a wide berth, just as they had for Silvia.

"Okay, everyone!" Gideon yelled to get the group's attention.

Eli sat where he had before. Brynlee, Wayne, and Joseph were sitting in a row next to Silvia. Travis kept glaring at Wayne.

"As you can see, we have some visitors today. You three introduce yourselves," Gideon said.

Brynlee stood up immediately, followed by Joseph and Wayne. "I'm Brynlee," Brynlee said, looking stonily at everyone in League Four like she wanted to slit all their throats.

After Wayne and Joseph introduced themselves, they all sat. "Kayla has some news from the raid," Gideon said.

Kayla's face reddened, and she shrank in her chair. Eli felt heat in his stomach again at the way Gideon was making his team mortify themselves. Everyone turned their attention to Kayla, except for Eli. Kayla shakily got to her feet as several people slumped in their seats. She grimaced and started talking, telling of the gruesome ways that their teammates had died. Tears streamed down her face, and her ears turned red. She sat down and looked at her lap. People were muttering to each other.

"Now—" Gideon started.

"Hey! I have a question!" Eli cut in, his fury getting the better of him. He felt himself rise in his seat a bit.

Gideon's attention snapped to his younger brother. "Now's not the time, brother."

"Well, I don't care!" Eli said hotly.

"Eli," Bryce whispered.

Eli stood up, ignoring his roommate. "Why do you always make the people who were at the event tell the story in front of the whole group, embarrassing them? Why don't you tell a story for a change?"

"Eli," Gideon said warningly.

"Why don't you go on raids yourself?" People started whispering, and Gideon's face turned scarlet. "Why don't we all go in one raid? So, we don't have to recount what happens? Why don't you go and risk your neck like everyone else? Don't you care about anyone?"

Gideon stood up. People were whispering, and some were nodding at Eli, encouraging him to continue.

"Eli, come," Gideon said imperiously.

"No," Eli said.

"Eli," Bryce whimpered, shrinking in his chair.

"Don't you care about Mom?" Eli dared.

People gasped.

"What was that about MaKenzee?" someone asked, standing up.

Gideon's eyes sparked as he stormed over to Eli. He grabbed him by the arm and forced him out of the chair.

"Hey!" several people protested.

Gideon dragged Eli out of the room as if he were a misbehaving toddler and slammed him to the wall. "You shut your mouth! Don't you think I'm already doing my best to protect and to get the job done?"

"No," Eli said, his eyes fixed upon Gideon's

"You shall not talk for the rest of the meeting."

"Is there a problem with the so-called master?"

Both brothers broke their gazes and looked to the door. Brynlee stood there with her dagger out, giving Eli a sympathetic look.

"Thought your scrawny figure might need some help. Nice big brother." She walked back into the meeting room.

"We are not finished," Gideon growled, baring his teeth and glaring at Eli. He stood up straight and stormed back into the meeting room. Eli rubbed his arm and followed.

The room filled with an angry buzz when Eli sat down again. A hand shot up, and Gideon called on the person who raised it.

"Eli's right," they said. "Why shouldn't the whole league attack at once? We could overthrow them that way, especially if League Two joins us. Everyone together."

"That would be suicide," Gideon said.

"Ha! You call that suicide? What about sending a group of four teenagers into a heavily armed base without even going yourself?"

There were murmurs of agreement.

"Why don't we do it together?" another person asked. Suddenly the room erupted with speech. People got together in groups and started planning strategies. Gideon glared at them, then stormed out of the room. Norah followed him.

Eli looked around, stunned at what his anger had done to people. He looked in Mia's direction. She was smiling at him, but when she noticed his gaze on her, she quickly turned and engaged in conversation with Harper.

"Dude," Bryce said, sitting stunned beside him. "You should take Gideon's place. You seem to have leader power."

Eli looked around the room again. Kayla had slumped down in her chair, and Brynlee, Wayne, and Joseph were actually talking, plotting with a group of people. There were many other groups now spread about the room, discussing excitedly. Several people still sat in their chairs, however, arms folded, glaring at Eli as though they disapproved of him. Ten minutes later, someone gathered everyone around the table again just as Gideon burst into the room, Norah right behind him.

Gideon's rage was evident. "Good! I can see you are all ready to settle down to have a civilized meeting."

"We have a plan," a rather brave woman said, standing up.

Gideon glared at her. "I never issued a full-league battle."

"No. But you never issued a double-league battle," the woman said, smiling over at Brynlee, Joseph, and Wayne.

Gideon sat down, staring daggers at her. Each group commenced in sharing their ideas, and soon the whole table buzzed with excitement.

"Fine!" Gideon bellowed. "Fine! We shall take the next two days to prepare for this undignified siege. Brynlee, Joseph, and Wayne, you three can go and inform your group about the plan. *Go.*" The three stood up. "Harper, Mia, lead them out."

Eli looked nervously at Harper, but Harper understood. She jerked her chin up as if to say, *I've got this. Mia will be okay.*

~

"So, when did you become so good at persuasive speeches?" Bryce asked.

Eli stammered, "Uh…I don't know."

"Well, it's useful. Hopefully, no one dies in two days."

"Oh. Thanks for reminding me of that possibility."

The two were lying on their beds, staring at the ceiling.

"It'd be nice if—" Eli stopped himself. "Never mind."

"If you could convince Mia to have a crush on you?" Bryce teased, grinning.

"Shut up."

Chapter 12

M ia, I can't help but tell you…"

"Tell me what?" Mia looked at him, and her eyes sparkled.

"I - I love you, Mia. I don't want to be without you."

"I love you too, Eli." Mia held out her hands. Eli took both of them and drank in her gaze.

"I am never going to forget this moment. Will you be my girlfriend?"

Mia's smile lit her whole face as if a spotlight was shining down on it. "Yes, of course, I will, Eli!" She hugged him close.

Eli opened his eyes to the white ceiling of his room. He shook his head and looked around for Mia. Bryce's bed was empty. He sat up and sighed, realizing that what he hoped had happened was only a dream. He lay back on his bed; his bones were dead tired from yesterday's events. He reluctantly got out of bed and got dressed.

He stepped into the hallway and looked both ways. No one was there. He started walking down the hall, his footsteps echoing. He turned a corner and spotted Mia walking towards him. His heart raced, and his mind replayed his dream at lightning speed. He could tell her now. There was no Bryce or Harper to laugh at him. She continued approaching him. *It's now or never.* He felt himself start to shake, and his stomach fluttered uncomfortably as the distance between them shrank. Her face held no expression.

"Gideon sent me to find you," she said in a flat tone. Then she did a double-take. "What's up, Eli?"

His stomach flipped when she said his name. "I…uh…umm…" His brain blanked. A ringing resounded in his ears. "Nice day out," he squeaked.

Mia looked around the windowless corridor. "Are you okay?" she asked, tilting her head sideways just enough to make Eli's mind go wild.

"You're gorgeous," he slurred out. His eyes filled with black dots.

"What did you say?" Her voice seemed distant. "Eli?" She was shouting his name. "Eli! Eli!"

He opened his eyes to find himself on the cold floor. Mia hovered over him with a worried expression. He sat up, then felt dizzy. He lay down again.

"Eli, what's wrong with you?" she asked. He blinked and took several deep breaths. "You passed out." He couldn't help but be self-conscious about her hands on his back, helping him up as she kneeled beside him.

"Um." He shook his head, and it cleared slightly. He did not feel like talking, but he wanted to say something to her.

"What happened? You saw me, and your face turned scarlet."

Eli felt sick. He stood up, despite his shaking body, and started walking away.

"Eli!" Mia called after him, frustrated. He just kept walking. His ears were flaming hot. Mia ran up to him. "What did you want to tell me?"

His face flushed again, and he averted his gaze.

"*Boys*," he heard Mia mutter in exasperation.

Eli stopped. "Mia," his voice squeaked. He grimaced at his stupidity. *Why is it so hard to ask a girl to be my girlfriend? They're just girls. Nothing to be afraid of... Well, unless the girl is Mia or Brynlee. Just my luck.*

"Yes?" she asked. She seemed unusually interested in what he had to say, giving him the slightest hope.

"I, um... I've been thinking—"

"There you are! Where have you been?" Bryce clattered down the staircase behind him. He spotted Mia and halted, his eyes widening as he realized what was going on. "Oh. Never mind."

Bryce turned to leave. Just then, Harper came down the steps. Bryce stopped and motioned to Harper. Her mouth formed an O. She turned and left with Bryce.

"You've been thinking about what?" Mia had a hair stuck to one of her eyelashes.

Eli shakily reached out and brushed it out of her face. Mia just stood there like nothing had happened. "I um…"

"Just spit it out, will you?"

Eli felt his stomach jerk inside himself. *I can't do it!*

"Never mind." He turned and ran out of the hall, up the steps, and right into Bryce, who stood just outside the doors that lead to a large room.

"So, did you do it?" Bryce asked Eli.

"Do what?" Eli asked.

"Tell Mia you like her." Bryce stated the obvious.

"Oh, um…"

"He chickened out," Mia said, as she walked through the doorway. Eli looked after her as she continued on acting like she had never seen them. Harper rushed to catch up with her.

"What?" Bryce asked.

"I did not tell her anything," Eli said. The back of Mia's straight hair waved back and forth as she walked.

"It must have been completely obvious," Bryce said.

"Or she heard you say what you just said a second ago," Eli

grumbled to himself.

Bryce looked disappointed. "Dude, this is getting ridiculous."

"Dude, be quiet and stop butting in on me!"

"Dude." The voice from behind them made the two jump. They turned to see Gideon and Norah standing before them. "I've been looking for you. It's one o'clock."

Eli stared at his brother. *I hope Gideon didn't hear any of that.*

"Come," Gideon beckoned. "We must plan the attack. You will be the leader of a group."

Eli felt the blood rushing from his head. "I... I'm not leading the attack, am I?" He tried not to let his voice shake.

"Yes. It was your idea, after all."

"Doesn't a good leader usually lead the battles?" Eli challenged.

Bryce stepped back nervously. "Dude," he whispered.

Gideon clenched his fist, but Norah put a hand soothingly on his shoulder. "Gideon," she purred. "It's okay. Let's just go get this done."

Gideon looked at her and nodded.

~

"So, let me get this straight, I came up with the idea for this attack, and even though I feel like I have only lived here for a day and a half, I am going to be leading this large attack on Base One? When I know almost nothing about what we are up against? When no one has been able to defeat League One in centuries? Is that right?" Eli asked Gideon, who had just finished explaining to him what he was about to do.

"Yes," Gideon said simply.

"Oh, great, just wanted to clear that up," Eli said.

Norah started to say something, but Gideon interrupted her.

"You and the others can go through our armory and start picking your weapons. We will attack the day after tomorrow, at sunrise. The sooner, the better."

~

"Hey, Bryce, if I don't make it out tomorrow...tell Mia that I enjoyed knowing her for the time I knew her, and um... Yeah, the other thing."

Eli and Bryce were going through the league's weapons the next day. It was early morning, and Eli felt he had to say something.

Bryce grinned at Eli. "I sure will, but maybe I will have Harper say it. Mia goes easier on girls than she does on us guys."

Eli rolled his eyes. "I'm an idiot."

"You are not, dude!"

"Dude is not a what?"

Both boys looked around. Harper and Mia were at the doors to the armory, apparently coming to do the same thing they were.

"Nothing," Eli said quickly. He turned away.

The four had been sorting in silence for a few minutes when Eli had a thought so magnificent that he nearly knocked Harper out by dropping a large shield.

"Watch out!" Mia yelped.

"Guys, if we attack League One, League Three is sure to attack too, and we might end up killing people on our team. My mom was on their team, after all... We can't let that happen!"

"How are we going to figure out who from our team is on their team in less than twenty-four hours?" Bryce asked.

"I don't know exactly. But I have an idea," he said.

"What?" Bryce prompted.

"I do what I did to my mom..."

"How is she?" Harper asked.

"I don't know."

"What do you mean? What did you do to your mom?" Mia asked.

"I knocked off her helmet... By mistake. We could do the same thing to the rest of League Three."

"How?"

"I guess flying," he said with a shrug.

"League Three has a lot of guards around their base... I've seen them many times," Mia commented. "But most of them have helmets."

"When should we go and find out?" Bryce asked.

"As soon as we're done, I think," Eli said gravely. "Before I lose my nerve."

~

"Okay. So, so...um...yeah." Eli shifted awkwardly.

The four had snuck out of their base and were a few blocks away from League Three's base. Eli's stomach started trembling yet again with nerves.

"Once we find who is in our league, how do we get them back on our side?" Harper asked.

"Good question..." Mia's face turned pale. "I have an idea, though."

"What?"

"Uh...get one of their guns and...shoot them, so they forget."

"Mia! How could you think of that?" Harper asked.

"How else are they going to get on our side again? Have them wake up in the middle of armed forces, then we move in and say we are there to rescue them or something."

"We will be overpowered. And how will we get our hands on one of their guns?" Bryce asked.

"I have one," Mia said in a small voice. All their mouths gaped open.

"You what, Mia?" Bryce asked.

Mia reached into a back pocket and pulled out a gun with three red stripes on it.

"Mia," Eli breathed, staring at the gun.

She flinched when he said her name so softly. "I got it from Harper."

Everyone looked at Harper.

"Remember when Br-" Harper did not finish. She did not need to.

"Yes," Eli said. Everyone stared at the gun in awed silence.

"Well…" Mia finally said. "Let's do this."

"Let's get our parents back," Eli said, feeling sick.

Harper put her hand on his shoulder. "You can do it," she said, looking right into his eyes with confidence. He nodded sullenly back at her. She stepped back and looked at Bryce, whose eyes lingered on her longer than they normally might have.

"Hey." Mia put her hand on Eli's shoulder, just as Harper

had done. He tried not to recoil or blush in shock. "It'll be okay; I've got your back."

Eli's stomach seemed to take off and sail into the air all by itself.

Chapter 13

Eli took one last look at his friends, and Harper nodded solemnly at him. He took a deep breath, looked up, and pushed himself into the air. The substance that was breathable whizzed through his hair, making it ripple. He soared up so high that his ears should have exploded by the speed of his acceleration. White fluff encompassed him when he looked down, but Eli could still see the brick wall holding them in like hostages in a pen. Eli angled his height so that he was lying on his stomach in mid-air. All the bases were in sight, even the spot where the strange creature had come from. The guards of League Three surrounded their base. The helmets glinted in the light. Eli hovered there for several minutes, giving his friends time to get a good vantage point.

Eli saw places he had never seen before. League One, Two, Three, and Four. League One's base was the only base that looked different from the top. He could barely spot the movements of guards from the top of their base, and a cold trickle of sweat slid down his forehead as he thought about what the next day might bring. He worried that he would be too slow or that someone would look up and see him. He had no wish to meet Mia again without his memory.

He aimed at a helmeted head and zoomed down. He was so

157

fast that, as he'd hoped, only the person he aimed at noticed him. He snatched the helmet off and bolted up again. The person started and looked around. A few bored guards glanced at the person and jerked as well, staring at their bare face.

Eli waited for a gunshot, but nothing came. He tossed the helmet away and darted down again. He did this repeatedly as the guards got more and more confused and restless with every helmet he took. Several guards pulled guns to the ready, their eyes scanning the scene before them.

A *bang* rang out, and the person whose helmet Eli had just taken off collapsed. Eli looked down but was too high up to see who they were. He heard shouts. He whizzed down and up so fast that his stomach started to feel like a whirlpool.

When all the helmeted people were unhelmeted, he landed dizzily in the alley that he had launched from. He stumbled against the wall and leaned against it; he could hear shouts, screams, and more gunshots. He knew he should go help, but he could barely take a steady step. Talking and confused noises were coming around the corner. He pressed himself to the stone wall, breathing heavily.

Around the corner came Harper, who had a bloody lip, Mia, whose hair was messed up but otherwise seemed unhurt, and Bryce, who had many cuts on his arms and legs and held his nose. There were three other people with them.

"Who—" Eli was cut off as Harper held out her hand.

"We need to get them to base before they can escape from us."

"Who are you?" one of the women asked.

"Where am I?" the man said, confused.

Eli took Harper's hand, and they vanished.

~

They startled Gideon and Norah so badly that Norah fell out of Gideon's lap where she had been lying half on him and half on the couch. The three new people blinked in uncertainty.

"Gideon," Mia said. Gideon jumped to his feet.

"Ahem. Where have you been?" Then he seemed to notice the three new adults as Norah picked herself up off the floor. "Where did you find them?"

The adults looked at Gideon warily.

"League Three," Eli said, trying to make his voice sound casual and not give away how sick he felt. He wobbled a bit, and Harper steadied him.

"But, but—" Gideon stuttered.

"We decided to go on a rescue mission before our attack," Bryce said. Mia glared at him.

"Rescue mission? From where? For who?" the new man asked.

Gideon walked towards him. The man stepped back,

159

unsure of what to do.

"Liam," Gideon said. Both women and the man stared at Gideon like he had gone crazy.

"Who?" the man asked.

"Did you three lose your memory, too? I'm done with this stupid charade!" Gideon glared at the three teens. The adults skittered into a frightened huddle.

Mia stepped forward and held out the gun.

Gideon recoiled. "Don't you aim that thing at me!"

"I'm not *aiming it.*"

"Gideon's losing it," Eli muttered to Harper. He turned to Bryce, who was still clutching his nose and rapidly draining of color. "Dude, you okay?" "Umm...I don't think so." His voice came out all muffled.

"You should go get yourself cleaned up."

Bryce nodded, swayed dangerously, and scuttled off. Harper hurried after him. Eli turned back to Gideon, who seemed overwhelmed.

"Who are you?" the man, Liam, asked, stepping forward bravely.

"You are on our team. You were caught and kidnapped," Norah said, her gaze going to the other two women.

"Umm..." The adults looked as stunned as Eli had been

when he had first woken up.

~

"Well, that went well," Harper said. She and Eli sat in chairs by Bryce's hospital bed. He had broken his nose in a scuffle. It was taped up now, making him look almost like he had a stick growing out of his nose.

"Well? You call this *well?*" Bryce asked, pointing to his nose.

"Well, as well as we could have hoped. We rescued three of our teammates!" Harper said, squeezing one of Bryce's hands. Eli eyed the two suspiciously.

"Yeah," Eli said sullenly.

"What's up?" Harper asked him.

Just then, Mia walked into the ward. "How are you, Bryce?"

"Alive," Bryce answered.

"I'm glad about that." She sat down and looked at her hands.

"Mia, I—" Eli stopped himself. His eyes slid past Bryce to a bed on the other side of the ward, where the woman with long brown hair lay on a bed.

"Go see your mom. As far as I know, you have not been able to introduce yourself properly," Harper said kindly.

"Mia, I...I'm sorry that we did not find your parents," Eli

said quietly. She looked at him, and he was startled to see tears in her eyes.

"It's not your fault," Mia said.

He got up and squeezed past the others, unable to stop himself from "accidentally" brushing Mia's shoulder with his hand. She didn't jump away like he knew she would have if she knew he had done it on purpose.

It was as if his soul no longer remained in him as he walked to the woman who was lying in the bed, staring at nothing. Her arm was bandaged up well. The medics were running on double time to get everyone up and out for the next day's attack.

"Mom?" Eli asked, pulling up a chair so that he was close to her. She turned her head to look at him and gave a sad smile.

"Eli," she said.

"You remember me?"

"No. Gideon told me all about you."

Eli shifted uncomfortably, wondering what his brother would have come up with. "I'm glad we found you, um, you found us."

"I found you?" she asked. She reached out and brushed some brown hair off Eli's forehead. He closed his eyes. He had never felt—to his memory—his mom touch him before.

She grabbed his hand and managed to sit up fully. "I'm sorry that I left you."

"You did not mean to," Eli said. "It was the other side that took you from us. Do you know anything about Dad? Mia's parents?"

"Who is Mia? Dad? I have no clue who he was."

Tears filled his eyes. He stood up to go.

"Eli." His mom's voice made him halt.

"Yeah?" he asked in a husky voice.

"I'm glad you brought me here."

He smiled and turned to go.

"Love you," she said, making him halt again. He had never heard anyone say that to him in his living memory.

"Love you too, Mom," he said. He hurried out of the ward, his eyes stinging with tears.

~

"Eli." Eli closed his eyes in exasperation at Gideon's voice. He shut the door to the sick room.

"What?" Eli asked unenthusiastically. "Norah's not here."

"I did not come looking for her," Gideon said, stopping a few feet from Eli. His face did not look like his normal firmness; it was as if he were mulling something over inside his head. "I need to talk to you."

"You are." Eli was not in the mood to talk to his older brother right now.

"No, come with me." Eli rolled his eyes as he turned to follow Gideon, who walked briskly down the hallway heading to "Gideon's Chamber." Eli stopped beyond the chair. Gideon faced his seat, his back towards Eli.

"You don't remember Dad." It was a statement.

"No, how could I?"

"He was a leader."

"What are you getting at? Bragging that you inherited his leader role?"

"He was not the leader of the whole league!" Gideon whipped around, and Eli saw lines in Gideon's face.

"Gee, wow." Eli stepped back. "Can I go now?"

"You are a great conversationalist," Gideon sarcastically spat. Gideon abruptly got creepily calm. "I'm trying to tell you something important, brother."

Eli looked off, bored with his brother's conversation style.

"You don't remember Dad at all?"

"No. Apparently, my memory was somehow magically wiped."

Gideon twitched in frustration. "Mom always called you Eli, but she had told me that, one day, she wanted you to know your real name."

Eli stared. "Oh, so you're being sentimental now?"

"I'm only telling you this now because who knows what will happen tomorrow." Eli's stomach jolted inside his chest.

"Thanks for the reminder, I could die tomorrow," Eli turned and started walking towards the door, disgusted with his brother, not understanding why he and his brother could not get along.

"Dad's name was Elijah." Gideon's voice echoed around the room. Eli halted, this little bit of information on his dad sparking a spot of interest in his cluttered mind. He turned to face Gideon.

"Elijah?"

"Mom named you after dad; your full name is Elijah." Gideon's voice was full of an unexplainable hurt.

"Okay…" Eli trailed off, seeing Gideon's muscles tighten.

"I may have inherited your so-called leadership from dad, but you got his name. Something that will live on forever, while my role will eventually die either with me or move to someone else." Eli's eyes stayed on his brother, trying to determine why his brother was so angry and resentful towards him.

"Well, thanks for letting me know." Gideon's resentment seemed to be leaking onto the floor and slowly seeping its way into Eli's feelings that were already in a scramble. Eli left, leaving his brother looking after him.

"Eli," Eli ignored his brother.

~

"Eli."

Eli kept walking down the corridor, trying to catch his breath and compose himself again. Everything in his life was messed up.

"Eli!"

The touch on his shoulder made him turn, his heart racing when he saw who was behind him. Mia. She never, *never* hunted him down on purpose unless she had to.

"What does Gideon want now? We just talked," he asked, blinking hard.

"Nothing." Mia looked slightly hurt.

"Then what?"

"I don't know."

He stared at her, waiting for more.

She shifted. "It's just that…I guess… You've changed."

"Okay…is that good or bad?"

"Good, I mean, you are still kinda an idiot, and no denying you were a major idiot before, but you stopped pranking me. I appreciate that."

Eli had no clue what to say. "Why would I prank you? I don't even know what that is."

With that, she burst out laughing and bent over, chuckling. Eli noticed the fluorescent light glinting off her hair. His stomach fluttered.

She straightened up. "Well, that settles it!" Mia said. He felt a bit more relaxed now. "You are still an idiot! But a—"

Eli had no idea what she was getting at. *Girls,* he thought. "Um, so…"

"Yeah. That's what I wanted to tell you."

"That I'm an idiot?"

She punched his shoulder, just like old times—or just like a few days ago. It actually kinda hurt.

"That you changed." She smiled at him, revealing bright white teeth.

His hands got clammy. He stepped forward, staring into her eyes. She noticed him step forward and looked a little scared. He took another step and shakily touched her arm with his hand. He started leaning forward.

"What's up, guys?"

Eli jumped and stepped so that he stood next to her.

Travis walked towards them, hand in hand with Silvia.

"Nothing," Eli said quickly.

"Nothing?" Travis asked, looking with raised eyebrows at Eli's left hand. With a start, he realized that he had grabbed

Mia's hand without realizing it. Apparently, she had not noticed—or minded? He hoped that she did not mind. He liked it. When she realized what Travis meant, she snapped her hand free and raced out of the room in a blur. Eli's face burned with embarrassment.

Travis grinned. "Winning her over?"

"I'll see you at dinner," Eli said matter-of-factly.

"Hey, you got this, man," Travis said, grinning broadly. Silvia smiled up at Travis. Travis continued, "Eli-"

But Eli had turned on his heels and left at a brisk pace.

~

"I'm always interrupted!" Eli complained to Bryce that evening at dinner.

"I don't know what to tell you. At least she doesn't tear your guts out anymore."

"Ew," Harper said.

Just then, Travis and Silvia joined their table.

"So...getting a little comfortable with someone in particular?" Travis asked Eli.

Eli looked at him and shrugged.

"Ready for tomorrow?" Harper asked, saving him.

"No, I'm not ready to make more people die," Kayla said. She sat next to Eli and kept passing him a drink as soon as he was halfway done with the last. He started feeling all jittery, even with Kayla's drowsy presence.

"You couldn't have done anything better," Harper insisted.

Mia came over to the table and sat next to Kayla. Eli immediately sat up straighter and felt his heart race. Travis looked at him pointedly. Eli rolled his eyes at him. Travis smiled and gave him the chin-up: *it's cool, man.*

"I'm scared." Everyone looked at Silvia.

"Why?" Bryce asked.

Mia snorted. "I wonder why, Bryce," she said sarcastically.

"I've never been in an attack before; I don't know what I'm doing." She looked at Travis with tears in her eyes. "I don't want to hurt anyone, but I don't want to die either."

Travis glanced at Eli as if to say, *This is how it's done, man.* Travis faced his girlfriend. "It's going to be okay." He wiped some tears away with one of his thumbs. "We will get through this. I have seen you fight; you're one of the best girl fighters I know." He put his chin on her head, pulling her close.

"Ahem." Mia coughed.

"I said one of the best," Travis said, correctly interpreting Mia's disgruntled sound.

"Brynlee is pretty tough," Eli commented, then regretted it. He had momentarily forgotten that Mia was at the table.

"That girl," Mia huffed. "We don't even know her blessing. How are we supposed to plot properly without knowing what she or Joseph can do?"

"We will find out tomorrow. Gideon talked to me earlier. Um, you and I are going to be leaders of a group of people our age, and that trio is in our group," Eli said.

"Oh, great," Mia moaned. "I have to share a leadership role."

"She's great at that," Bryce whispered to Eli with sarcasm.

"I heard that, Bryce. *And* I am working with someone who wants my throat to run red."

"Well, I will make sure that it does not," Eli said, putting his utensils down and looking over at Mia. Travis smirked at him.

"You're doing great," Bryce whispered. Harper elbowed him. "Hey!"

"Knock it off with the unhelpful relationship comments," Harper hissed so that only Bryce and Eli could hear. Kayla was too busy looking into her food with sadness to pay much attention to what was going on.

"I don't know. I don't want to lead a raid again…" Kayla trailed off. She stood up. "See you tomorrow, bright and early." She left the room, leaving an awkward gap between Eli and Mia.

Eli was self-conscious about the foot of space between

himself and her. His heart played a strange tempo in his chest. He noticed Bryce's smirk, Harper shooting him a look. Travis got up even though his tray was still half-full. Silvia followed his lead. Harper glanced at Eli's shifty and nervous body, pushed Bryce out of his seat, and forced him to move away.

"Hey!" Bryce protested but eventually left with Harper.

There was silence at the table. Mia seemed to know what her friends had done to her and looked slightly wounded that they would leave her here with Eli.

"So, ahem." *Why does my voice have to squeak?*

Mia looked at him with raised eyebrows. "Don't think earlier today changed anything," Mia said.

"Earlier today?"

She did not answer, but her right hand twitched, and he got the message. He looked over to where Harper and Bryce were scraping their leftovers into a trash can. Bryce took one last look over at them, grinning, then Harper shoved him out of the room. People were still buzzing all around them.

"Um, so what are your plans for the raid tomorrow?" He felt stupid for asking the question.

"I don't know," Mia said stiffly.

He shifted and sat on his hands, refusing to let them do what he wanted them to. Her right hand was right there, next to her plate, empty. "I have—" He cleared his throat again. *Stupid pitch.* "I have an idea."

She looked at him, and he shuffled his feet. "Yeah?" Her eyes glinted even in this light! Why did she have to be so stubborn?

"Our group could surprise them by starting on the roof." He got a vision of the strange thing and heard its *roof!* again. Tears sprang to his eyes, and he quickly tried to wipe them away, but Mia noticed.

"Hey, what's wrong, Eli?" *Why did she ask that? She hates me.* He shook his head. "Tell me," she insisted.

He started to grab his plate, but she put her hand on his wrist to stop him from leaving. *Yes!* He sat down again and stared at his plate, noticing that her hand was back where it had been. *I can tell Mia, right? She would understand why no one else but her could know... She is Mia, after all.*

"When we went looking for a meeting place, there was this thing," Eli said.

She looked at him curiously. "Thing?"

"Yeah, it was a thing like Gideon changes into but a whole lot smaller. It made this funny sound and seemed happy to see us. It led us to the wall and—" He stopped. The fresh smell came back to his nose again. He could see the too-brightness of the other place and the green things.

"And?" Mia prompted.

"And we saw - Harper, Bryce, and I saw…" And suddenly, he got the feeling that Harper must have had when they had seen it. He saw the bright colors again; he saw the things he had never seen or dreamed really existed, and something inside him overflowed. He put his head in his hands. He became overwhelmed with the memory; he could see the thing dancing in that beautiful green, a lighter shade than his suit. His shoulders shook with sobs.

"Eli." Mia's voice quieted. He could tell that she was staring at him. He looked up and brushed the tears away.

"There was—" His throat had a large lump clogging it. "I don't know how to describe it. There was a hole in the wall."

"What?" Mia asked, scooting back in surprise.

"There was a spot where the brick had crumbled away. The thing went through it, and when I looked…" He stared off into space. "There was green, pink. Colors coming from where the concrete should be. The sidewalk was slightly above the green. The green was everywhere, and brown things were coming up or down from the green, leaving funny shadows on the ground. It was so bright that I could barely see up high. I did not want to tell anyone about it, but how can I not tell you?"

Mia shifted uncomfortably. "You never used to say things like this to me," she said in a quiet voice. "What happened?"

"I don't know," he said honestly. "I don't fully understand why I was not like this before."

They stared at each other, then Gideon's voice told everyone to pick up their table, and Eli and Mia broke their gaze. It had made Eli slightly uncomfortable; she had never looked at him with such a calculating expression before.

~

"So...how'd it go?" Bryce asked Eli when he found Bryce and Harper sitting in a nook together.

"What?" Eli had been lost in thought about the thing and the outside world. *What was it like?*

"Um...Mia," Bryce prompted, raising his eyebrows.

"Oh." Eli sat down in an armchair.

"What's up? Did you—" Harper jabbed Bryce in the ribs.

"Oof."

"I couldn't help it," Eli confessed. "I told Mia about the hole in the wall."

The two looked shocked.

"Eli!" Bryce said. "You told us not to tell anyone!"

"I know... But I just can't help but feel it's important. There's something strange about that hole; it doesn't just randomly appear."

"Yes, it does. After so many years, stuff is bound to disintegrate. It's natural," Bryce said.

"But what if..." Eli trailed off. His mind seemed to be

billowing up, stretching to the seams. *What if the hole has something to do with the brick? What if... What if...*

Eli insisted, "It has something to do with tomorrow; I can feel it."

Chapter 14

Eli woke with a jolt. A loud, buzzing call rang through the building. Bryce sat up and groggily rubbed his eyes. Eli's stomach filled with dread. He bent over, clutching his stomach, and gasped.

"You okay, dude?" Bryce asked in a hoarse voice as he climbed down his ladder in a more careful way than usual.

"Yes," Eli lied, rubbing his stomach that churned like two whirlpools going in different directions. He stumbled down the ladder, missing the last step as he fumbled to regain his balance.

The two left their room. Eli had the uncomfortable thought that it might be the last time he would ever see it again. He and Bryce started walking down the hall when the alarm finally stopped. Travis came out of a room not too far down the hall from them. He jogged to catch up with them.

"This could be the day," he said, twiddling his thumbs.

"It was a lousy idea," Eli said, staring right ahead of him.

"No! It's got to work!" Travis insisted.

Eli looked at Travis, realizing that he had said that out loud. Down the hall, Mia and Harper came out of their room. Mia's hair seemed especially shiny this morning. Eli slowed his walk and fell behind the others, trying to stay away from Mia even though he wanted to be close to her. He thought she could soothe his boiling nerves, but he knew that she would have none of that. None at all.

Bryce looked back to see where he had gone. Eli jutted his chin up. The others left the hall. He stopped and pressed his back against the cold wall. His breath came out rapidly as he slid down so that his head rested on his knees. He hyperventilated and tried not to cry—an eighteen-year-old crying. Boys didn't cry; Gideon had made that clear to him in a meeting that they had together. *Boys should not be in a life and death situation like this their whole lives.* He stayed there, his face buried in his arms, fighting his writhing stomach and shakiness.

He felt a hand on his shoulder. He looked up with watery eyes to see a woman crouching down by him—his mom.

"You okay, honey?" She had quickly gotten used to the idea that she had kids, even if one was an arrogant leader.

Eli shook his head.

"Come here." She pulled him into a hug, and the tears broke through the dam. They poured down his face, making the back of her soft shirt damp with their saltiness. "Shh," she soothed, rubbing his back. She sat down on the floor and rocked him back and forth. "It's going to be okay."

"How can you know?" Eli whimpered. Her shirt muffled his voice.

"I don't," she whispered. "But it will be okay."

"I never should have come up with the idea." He hugged her tighter, thankful for someone who did not shy away from him or look nervous when he had uncontrollable emotions.

"That Mia is pretty smart, isn't she?" Eli looked up at her face. She gave him a sad smile. "I know how you feel about her. I see it in your face." He looked down, but she made him look at her. "You can think that you are doing this for her. For her protection."

"She is not the one who needs protection; it's me. She's…she's…" He could not finish. Mia was no doubt one of the best fighters and self-advocators he had ever known in his memory.

His mom hugged him again before standing and helping him up. "Sometimes, I think the people who act fierce are the people who need the most protection." He looked at her in surprise. "You'll get her." She smiled at him. "Don't you worry."

"I don't think you know her like I know her."

His mom laughed. "Are you a girl?"

"No."

"Then how do you know?"

"I'm an idiot." They started walking down the hall.

His mom laughed and pulled him into a side hug. "You are a smart young man, and I love you."

"I love you too, Mom."

~

"Everybody, group up!" Gideon's bellow jerked everyone to attention in the cafeteria later that morning. Eli had no appetite, but much to his annoyance, Harper and Bryce had forced him to eat something. Eli looked at the people surrounding the table who comprised his team. He felt like he might lose what little food he did eat.

"Where did you say our team from League Two was going to meet us again?" Bryce asked.

"Entranceway," Mia answered as she walked up to the table, ignoring Eli as usual.

"We should get going," Harper said. They all stood up, cleared their table, and started walking towards the entranceway along with half a dozen other groups who also looked nervous. They found a large group of people from League Two. Soon, Brynlee, Wayne, and Joseph stepped through the doors and walked up to Eli, Mia, Bryce, Harper and Kayla. Travis and Silvia joined them. Wayne's eyes darkened as he saw Silvia with Travis.

"Hey," Eli made himself say. His mouth seemed to have lost all its saliva. Brynlee glared daggers at everyone as Wayne jerked his head in a sullen *hey*. "So…we should go get our weapons."

Brynlee nodded. The group awkwardly followed Mia down the hall to the armory.

"Ready for today?" Eli asked Joseph.

"What?" Joseph asked. He blinked hard and looked at Eli.

"Oh...um, are you ready for today?" Eli asked again.

"Oh. Not really, but okay."

Eli nodded in agreement. Joseph seemed distracted. He kept on blinking and shaking his head as if to clear it.

"You okay, man?" Eli finally asked.

"It's normal," Joseph brushed off. Eli looked at him from the corner of his eyes. Joseph had his fingers to his temples as if trying to clear his brain. "Concentrate," Eli heard him whisper to himself.

They reached the armory door, and Mia pulled it open.

"Nice stash," Brynlee commented. She headed straight for the daggers that were hanging off the wall and selected a dagger belt. Joseph and Wayne looked on, unsure what to do.

"Help yourself," Eli encouraged. He had no idea what weapon would suit him. He hated the idea of touching one.

Mia just stood in the doorway. He approached her. "Hey." *How dumb could I sound? Hey?* "Um...what weapon are you going for?"

She continued to ignore him.

"Right." He started looking around. Swords didn't seem to suit him. No guns. He had seen too many of those recently...no daggers on chains, no whips. No nothing.

"I might just go in empty-handed. Use the brainpower I don't have," Eli said.

Brynlee flinched at the word *brainpower*. Once everyone had selected their weapons, Eli had unenthusiastically strapped a gold sword to his belt, feeling foolish. It seemed like he was pretending to be a swordsman with no idea how to use a sword.

He turned to the group. "So." All eyes were on him. "So, I think it would be beneficial for everyone to know all of our blessings. That way, we can use them to our advantage today." He swallowed hard. "Mine is flying."

Brynlee, Joseph, and Wayne stared at him. He turned to Mia with a pleading look.

"Some of you already know," she said with a sigh. "I can run."

Bryce snorted. "I'm good at boxing," Bryce said, bored.

"Sleet." Harper demonstrated by sending a puff of white stuff into the air from one of her hands. Joseph gazed at the fading sleet as if mesmerized.

"Sleep," Kayla muttered.

They looked to the three from League Two. Joseph shifted and shook his head.

"I don't know mine," Silvia said, looking, much to Wayne's annoyance, to Travis.

"You are flexible," he said, smiling at her.

Wayne clenched his fists.

"I can sing." Mia raised her eyebrows at Travis. "I'm joking; I sound like something shrieking when I sing."

Silvia giggled. Wayne's face turned sour.

"I seem to be okay at everything," Travis said, shrugging. "I can pick up a weapon I have never seen before and learn it instantly."

Brynlee looked at him with a little more respect than she usually showed League Four.

"Ahem. I—" Joseph cut himself off and squeezed his eyes shut. He opened them again and blinked hard. "I can see things that are not happening in front of me."

"Huh?" Harper asked.

He shook his head again as if to clear it. "I can see what's happening in other rooms—especially violence. It takes me away from the present."

"That's why he's so quiet," Wayne elaborated. "It's hard for him to be in two spots at once."

Brynlee glared at him.

"I'm good at throwing things," Wayne offered. "And I can silence people."

"Especially me," Brynlee put in.

"How about you?" Harper asked. Eli flinched. He knew better than to get on Brynlee's bad side.

"None of your business."

"Brynlee!" Joseph reproved sharply.

She rolled her eyes. "I can feel people's emotions," Brynlee said.

Eli immediately inched away from Mia. Brynlee's eyes dug into Eli. "Yeah, I know already," she said. "And not just from people I focus on. I can feel the emotions of everyone within three miles of me."

"That must be awful," Harper whispered. Brynlee twitched in annoyance.

Another group appeared at the door.

"Um, so let's go to a quiet room before both the leagues get together," Eli suggested.

"Okay," Joseph agreed. Brynlee glared at him. "Just somewhere quiet," he told her.

The group walked to Gideon's room, which was unusually empty. They stood in an awkward circle.

"Any game plans? We are one of the first groups to move in on the attack," Brynlee asked finally.

"We are the first," Mia said. Everyone paled.

"Oh," Wayne said, inching towards Silvia. Travis shot him

a look.

Brynlee's arm twitched. "Ugh. I feel rotten - all these emotions!"

Joseph looked uneasily at his sister. "She never complains about them," he whispered to Eli.

"Yeah, Wayne, give it up," Brynlee snapped at Wayne. Wayne stopped inching towards Silvia and glared at her.

"Give what up?" Harper asked.

"Do you have to ask? There are so many of the same emotions going on right now, and I hate it! If you could all just stop feeling...ugh!" She clutched her head.

"I can't stop feeling nervous even if I tried," Eli admitted.

"Not that!" Brynlee turned around in an exasperated circle. "A different feeling that, like, half of you are feeling."

They all looked at each other uneasily.

"Um..." Joseph shifted. "What do you mean?"

"*You* aren't feeling it, thank goodness!"

"Ohh! Is it...the feeling you hate?"

Brynlee glared at him, affirming his question. "My least favorite." She glared at Eli. "*You* are feeling it the strongest, and you are sure of it."

"Umm..." Eli stuttered.

"What?" Harper asked, confused.

"And you are a jealous version of it." Brynlee turned sharply to Wayne, who stepped back as if intimidated by his friend's ferocity. "And you two have it." She pointed accusingly at Travis and Silvia. She focused on Harper, and her eyes could have shot lasers like Addy's. She turned to Mia. "And you are confused and unsure of the feeling that is clearly there." Mia stepped back, looking somewhat frightened.

"About what?" Harper asked.

"No," Brynlee said, turning around.

Joseph looked at Eli with raised eyebrows. Silence.

"How about a pep talk?" Harper piped up. She turned expectantly to Mia.

Everyone else followed her lead. Eli noticed Bryce kept on glancing at Harper.

"Well... Do better... Do better than we have before," Mia told them.

Eli could tell that she was thrown off guard with what Brynlee had told her. *But what emotion was that?*

"Great," Harper said, clearly let down by Mia's helpful improv talk. They looked to Eli. He gulped and hoped that he would not break down again like he had this morning.

"I may not have known you long—a few days. I know it's been longer, but I can't remember. But in the few days that I remember knowing you all...I can't explain properly." He paused, feeling stupid. They were all watching him, even Mia. "I'm already ready to get out of here, but I would not trade knowing any of you for anything. Brynlee, I have not known you long, but I can tell that you are a courageous person who won't let people down. Joseph, you are a silent warrior. Literally. Wayne, you um...you have hair that stays in place no matter what is happening. Silvia, you are graceful and pleasant to be around."

With this, Travis pulled Silvia to him and gave Eli a sharp look. Brynlee glared at Travis.

"Travis. You are a great encourager. You help people get back on their feet when they are confused. Bryce, you welcomed my stupidity back and acted like we just met for the first time. Harper, you are such a good friend, and you can't be replaced."

He turned to Mia. "Mia." He stopped and blinked hard, trying to pretend that no one else stood there. "I woke up with you yelling at me. I had no idea who I was or who you were. You saved my life. And I...I feel something that I can't explain." Brynlee's face crumpled into exasperation. "I don't think that it's just because of that, but um..."

He trailed off, embarrassed. He looked over the group. Bryce was grinning at Harper, and Harper did her best to look anywhere but at Bryce. She shifted from foot to foot.

"We can do this. If we work together, we can win our freedom. Now let's go and show them what we're made of!" Eli had tried to make his voice sound defiant and encouraging at the end. They all stared at him in stunned silence.

"Right," Brynlee awkwardly said. "Let's let our captains have a last word before we go out there. C'mon, guys."

Everyone but Mia and Eli followed. The door swung shut. They stood in silence, then Mia started to walk towards the door.

"What did she mean?" Eli's voice broke the uncomfortable silence.

Mia stopped and stiffly turned around. "What did who mean?" she asked.

"What Brynlee said about you being unsure of a feeling. What feeling is that?"

"It's none of your business." She turned to go.

"But if we share the same feeling—" He cut himself off as she turned angrily and stalked toward him.

"I'm done talking about this."

Eli stepped back, but he had to know. "Is it about me?"

She leaned over him, her fists clenched. "Shut up."

"I'm just asking a question."

She slapped him in the face and stormed out the door. Eli felt his cheek where her hand had made contact with his skin. It felt raw from her force. He couldn't help but grin slightly as she stormed out of the room. He thought that he knew the answer to his unanswered question by her reaction. He took one last look around, and then Eli left to join the others.

~

When he reached his team, Mia was in deep conversation with Wayne and Harper. Brynlee raised her eyebrows at Eli as he approached the group.

"That's a better feeling," she said. "Less gushy. Disappointment is not as clogging." She raised her eyebrows further.

The alarm sounded, telling them the time had come.

Gideon stood up on a large chair near the entranceway. "This is it. This day could change our lives—permanently. We must fight our best and stay on top of everything. Group one approach."

Mia and Eli led their group to the doors towards Gideon.

"Brother, don't let me down."

Eli raised his eyebrows.

"No pressure," Brynlee whispered in his ear. A rustle broke through the crowd, and MaKenzee gave Eli a bear hug.

"You'll do great!" she said into his shoulder.

"Thanks, Mom," he said, slightly uncomfortable that she hugged him in front of the whole assembly. She turned to look at Gideon. He just stared at her with his strong *leader's eyes.* MaKenzee approached him for a hug, but he looked away.

"See you in a little while," he said. MaKenzee looked disappointed, but Norah, who stood behind him, stepped forward and hugged her. Eli's group left the building, circled up, and closed their eyes.

~

Eli opened his eyes. They were a few blocks from League One.

He turned to face the group. "Okay. So, here's the plan. I go up and scout around, then come back and take you all up to the roof. Kayla goes to the edges and puts the guards to sleep."

"Why can't we just teleport?" Brynlee asked.

"We don't want to appear unexpectedly on enemy territory, do we? We won't know exactly where to appear. Anyways, then we bust in and improvise from there."

"Great! My favorite type of crazy!" Wayne said. Brynlee glared at him. "What? Can't a guy crack a joke even when he faces death?"

Brynlee snorted. "Too many high emotions right now," she mumbled.

"Let's just get this done," Mia said. She looked at Eli. He let his eyes rest on her, ignoring everyone else.

"Well...in case we don't make it out of here alive..." He

held his hand out to her.

"We're not holding hands," Mia snapped. Harper raised her eyebrows at Eli as Brynlee screwed her face up.

"Well, okay then. Here I go." Eli shot up into the air.

The substance whipped through his hair and whistled in his ears. He went as high as he thought he could without being noticed and adjusted himself so that he was parallel to the ground. He circled above the base. It appeared close to the wall and had three layers of guards surrounding it to—*wait.*

The base seemed to end into the brick wall. *Huh? Does the base lead to the outside world?* He nearly fell out of the sky and started free-falling. He studied where the base's wall melted into the Wall. He shook his head and scanned the roof. There - a large chimney protruded in the middle, and a few guards were standing in front of it. The chimney was blocked from the top. He swooped down to the others and landed, winded.

"News?" Mia asked him stiffly.

"There are three lines of guards almost surrounding the building."

"Almost?" Brynlee asked.

"Yeah, um…the base appears to melt into the outside wall…"

"What?" Harper and Wayne asked sharply. They looked at each other and stepped back.

"Yeah," Eli said.

"What does that mean?" Bryce asked.

"I don't want to think about it." He once more saw the strange thing and heard its *roof!* "Are we ready?"

"No," Kayla said, clutching her stomach.

"Okay, who's coming first?"

"We can." Travis stepped forward with Silvia. Travis and Silvia each took one of Eli's hands. Eli took a deep breath. He could not remember trying to transport more than one person before. He shot up into the space of nothing. Silvia stifled a scream as they soared higher.

"My ears!" Travis groaned.

"Oh. Sorry. I forgot you guys can't go as fast." He slowed his travel.

Silvia looked down and whimpered. "So high."

"It's okay, babe," Travis said soothingly, though his hand shook in Eli's. It took Eli more brain power than usual to keep them steady. He tried to go down as fast as possible without attracting attention and set down right behind the chimney.

"Stay here," Eli hissed to them before shooting back down for the others. When they were all there, Eli turned to Kayla.

"Okay, it's your time," Eli said.

Kayla looked frightened. "I can't," she said, looking down.

"I can't lose all of you."

Eli put his hand on her shoulder. "You can. You can do more than you think."

She looked up at him with her eyes watering. She took a deep breath and handed one last energy drink to everyone before slipping around the chimney. Not long after, there were several thumps of guards falling to the ground. The sound of snoring disturbed the quiet morning.

"She's done it," Eli breathed. He motioned for the others to creep out from behind the chimney. They saw Kayla looking over the roof and concentrating on what was below. There once more came the slight clatter of armor as guards presumably fell asleep.

Eli and Joseph glanced at each other with amused expressions and took a sip of their energy drink simultaneously. They both cracked up and did their best not to let the drink spray out of their noses. Brynlee shot them a look and huffed. Kayla walked dazedly over to them once she had finished making a semicircle around the building's three guarded sides.

"Okay." She wobbled and almost fell. Harper caught and steadied her. Kayla blinked hard.

"You good?" Harper asked.

"Maybe." She pulled a bottle of Mountain Dew out of her pocket and drank the whole thing in a few seconds. "That's better." She summoned another and did the same.

"Okay. Let's give the signal," Eli said.

The group walked to the middle of the roof. Wane stepped forward and cupped his hands over his mouth. "Whoop whoop!" he called.

Nothing happened.

"Nice signal," Bryce commented.

Wayne grinned. "Thanks. I just made that up,"

The group approached the front edge of the building. They could see other groups emerging from alleys and creeping towards Base One. Eli caught a glimpse of his mom in the lead of one of them. He gave a swooping wave in her direction, and she waved back. He looked at his group.

"Ready?" he asked them. They all nodded.

Travis turned to Silvia and gave her a hug. "I love you," he told her.

"I love you, too," she said. Travis pressed his forehead against Silvia's.

Brynlee made a disgruntled sound. Eli cleared his throat.

"Okay, no pressure from my brother, but we are going to be the first group in," Eli said.

"Is it just me, or does it seem like your brother would not mind it if you got killed because he made us the first group and appointed you as one of the leaders?" Brynlee wondered.

Eli swallowed. "Um…I'm sure he would not mind." He glanced at Mia. "After all, I'm an idiot."

Mia managed a pained smile.

"Okay, let's do this," Eli said. "Three…two…one."

The group lowered each other to the ground. Eli was the last one down. Guards lay about, their heavy breathing the only reassuring thing about Eli's plan. He glanced over to see the rest of their combined teams awaiting their entrance. His group stepped to the front doors. Eli took a deep breath and flung them open.

Chapter 15

The group burst into League One's entranceway. The only sound they produced was made by Bryce; he had tripped over a doorstop. Eli shot Bryce a look; he shrugged.

They walked into the entrance hall that resembled League Four's and Two's.

Eli's nerves jangled. He couldn't relax. This was too easy.

Mia walked up to him and whispered, "What do you think? This can't be good."

Eli shook his head. "I dunno. Be ready for a surprise attack."

Mia passed the whispered message around as they continued creeping down the hall. Eli's heart thudded against his chest. The base was so quiet - too quiet. Eli glanced back behind him. Bryce and Harper didn't appear to be there. His eyebrows scrunched up in concern: *Why would they leave the group without telling anyone? Did Harper fall behind?* His stomach jolted. *Were they silently abducted? Was there a surprise attack coming for them?*

He observed the group, who was still progressing forward,

all their senses on alert. He should have heard any scuffles that broke loose. He fell behind slightly, glancing uneasily at Mia, who was now in the lead. *Why are they not here anymore?* It bugged him. He scanned the hallway, lined with doorways every few feet. He backtracked, peering into the rooms with open doors, being as stealthy as he could. Once he had gone about four doors down, his ears caught the sound of whispers.

"But what if one of us doesn't make it out?" Harper, worry overflowing in her voice.

"It's a *what if,* Harper." Bryce. Eli's eyebrows narrowed slightly.

"But if one of us dies-"

"Shh." Bryce's voice was surprisingly soft. Eli had never, in his memory, heard Bryce speak this way.

Eli peeked around the corner. Harper was standing inside; Bryce stood right in front of her.

Harper was trembling. "I don't know if I could live without you."

"It'll be fine." Bryce put his hand on Harper's cheek. Eli tucked back behind the wall, unwilling to let his friends see him spying on them.

"I - I can't do this, Bryce. I can't do it anymore. I can't."

"Hon-Harp, think about the green things, think about-about the *thing.*"

"I can't - I - I -" Harper's voice was choked with something wet as if she were crying.

Eli's pulse beat in his neck. He knew he shouldn't be here. *How can I interrupt politely?* This situation was worse than he had thought.

"Shh, can you tell me more?" Bryce murmured. There was a sound as if Harper was trying to talk. "It's okay."

"I'm - I'm done with this place."

They needed to move - what if some guards from the base strolled along and found them? This was not the place to have a breakdown, though he didn't blame Harper.

"What if - what if-" Harper's voice cracked.

Eli readied himself. He had to get them to catch up with the group, but he didn't know how to approach this. He took a deep breath and stepped into the doorway.

"Hey, guys, we should probably get going."

Harper and Bryce pulled apart from a hug.

"Eli." Bryce was trying to keep the guilt out of his voice.

"Eli's right; this is risky." Harper's voice shook, despite her trying to sound, and look, confident. "We need to go."

Eli felt like a terrible friend. He was self-conscious as he turned to catch up with the group, feeling lighter than he should be, as if he could lose his balance just by walking.

Embarrassment was sweeping through him in waves. *Had I interrupted something important?* But his nerves didn't like the quiet base any more than they had liked sneaking up and spying on Harper and Bryce. The three caught up with the group, who had reached the end of the hallway, right where it turned.

Kayla clutched her stomach. "Oh, no," she moaned.

Eli looked at her in concern. "What's wrong?"

"This is where— this is where—" Her eyes filled with tears.

She did not need to finish. This must have been where Layla, Wade, and Addy had died.

"It's okay," Harper squeaked to Kayla, giving her a quick hug.

"Yeah. No one is going to die today," Bryce said, eliciting stares from the group. "I'm just trying to be optimistic here."

"Shh!" Brynlee hissed. "I hear something."

They all paused to listen. There came a steady bleep, bleep, bleeping of a machine from a room with an open door. Brynlee led the way and peered inside.

"All clear," she whispered.

As Eli stepped into the room, the hairs on his neck stood on end.

"Something's not right," he hissed.

Kayla walked over to the machine. It was not very wide, but

it was a little taller than an average man, with some buttons and a flashing light. Kayla looked at the square screen. Everyone else but Eli hung back. The room had nothing else in it but the bleeping machine.

"Eli," Mia whispered as if she were nervous. He waved her off and walked over to Kayla. Kayla's eyes widened as she read the screen. Words kept on scrolling up. There were a few words in red. Kayla turned to Eli, wobbling like she was about to pass out.

"What?" Eli asked.

Her eyes were red, and tears streamed down her face. She motioned to the screen. He looked at it and was surprised to see that he could read the words. It had a list of names. Some of them he recognized from their league.

Layla Racent - Terminated

Addy Lactante - Terminated

Wade Hip - Terminated

Luke Armstrong - Terminated

Lily Armstrong - Terminated

Eliot Johnson - Terminated

Then, he came across something that nearly stopped his heart.

Elijah Johnson - Terminated

He clutched the side of the machine and gasped. His dad…

"Eli," Kayla said quietly. "I'm sorry."

Vision blurring, he read the name beneath his father's.

Eli Johnson - Wanted

His eyes drifted to the top of the screen where a line read: *Season 70, Episode 1.*

What? Season? Episode? What does that mean? But then his eyes drifted to the blood-red words near the top of the screen.

Mia Armstrong - Bait, just in case

Eli's legs gave out from under him. He hit the floor hard.

"Eli! What is it?" Harper rushed over.

"Bait?" he asked Kayla. Her eyes asked him to answer what was going on, to answer this apparent secret. "What does that mean?"

"I don't know, but—" Her voice wasn't loud enough to go over the sound of fighting that burst out.

While they were talking, people from League One had covered the entrance. Everyone had been too busy watching Kayla and Eli at the machine to have noticed. Eli turned at lightning speed to see Travis, Silvia, Brynlee, and Bryce in full combat with people in gold who were shoving their way into the room.

"Eli Johnson!" a booming voice bellowed over the loudspeaker.

A cold shiver passed through Eli.

"Protect M!" Eli shouted.

Mia glanced back at him in annoyance and ducked a blow from one of the men in gold. "I don't need protection, E!" she shouted at him.

"K, do your thing!" Eli ordered.

"But it'll make the others, too!" Kayla worried.

"That doesn't matter right now!" Eli said as he hurled himself into the fray. Joseph clutched his head in the background, seeming to be trying to clear his mind; Brynlee was stabbing one of the people who had jumped her.

"B! Enough! Be quick!" he roared at her. She glared at him before stabbing them one last time. She got up, and everything seemed to go in slow motion. Eli managed to disarm his attacker; Mia ran around the group and knocked one of the guys out, just in time for everyone to collapse on the ground, asleep.

~

Eli opened his eyes. Chaos danced around him. A tall girl with brown hair was yelling at him. Her hand slapped his dazed face. He felt her hand slip into one of his and pull him to his feet, hard.

"E!"

Everything came back to him. At least, everything from the past few days.

He shook his head and turned to see another wave of defenders surrounding them. But then, the other groups who had been waiting outside Base One entered the battle.

"We need to get out of here!" Eli shouted.

"You think?" Mia screamed at him as she dodged a bullet that smacked into the opposite wall.

"Let's go! H, keep an eye on M!" Eli ordered.

Harper gave him a strange look.

"Just do it!" he screamed.

The combined Leagues had done their job effectively. Few defenders remained. All at once, another wave of defenders seemed to materialize out of nowhere. Eli's fury boiled inside him now - the death stories of Addy, Layla, and Wade, the brick wall that surrounded them, the indignity of being forced into this *game* for his whole life. He swung with determination. Brynlee was an astonishing fighter. Taking down defender after defender, rarely hesitating to think. *She'll get the brick all by herself,* he thought to himself as she deflected a bullet that was aimed at Eli's head with her knife.

"Thanks," he panted.

"No probs!"

Wait, did she actually say you're welcome? He paid for his moment of distraction painfully. A bullet grazed his arm, and he fell to the floor, clutching the bloody wound.

"E!" Harper helped him to his feet.

He blinked away the dots that had sprung to his eyes. *Toughen up,* Mia's voice said in his head. He gritted his teeth and tried to stay alert. They were in the hallway that, at League Four, would lead to Gideon's chamber. Wayne had just tripped over something on the floor when an unusually loud bullet blast sounded. Wayne crumbled to the floor, blood trickling from the side of his head.

"*Wayne!*" Brynlee cried out in agony. She started toward him, but Eli caught her arm.

"Don't sacrifice yourself - don't give them an easy target!"

"*You are all easy targets,*" a voice came from over the intercom. Everyone stopped and looked around, even the people from League One. "*And thank you for walking into our base so that we can have some fun. Some of the episodes were getting um...boring.*"

Eli's stomach churned with anger. He looked right at the people who had the upper hand. He stepped forward, raising his sword. His arm ached. He did not want to kill anyone, but he had to hurt them at least to protect his friends and Mia. *Mia!* She was the one person on his mind for hours on end. She could not get hurt.

"Go!" he shouted to his group. "Into 'G's chamber—I'll

fend them off!"

"Oh, no, you won't!" Brynlee stepped next to him, anger carved on her face. The three people right in front of the two stood there casually as if they faced a mob of angry and frightened teenagers every day.

"You two won't either." Mia stepped next to him, and his heart lifted.

"But—"

"You really got 'em girls, dude!" Bryce's voice came.

"The rest of you, go!" Eli ordered.

The three charged. Eli was not exactly sure what happened. One moment himself, Brynlee, and Mia were standing in a defensive stance, and the next, Eli was running into the not-Gideon's chamber. He stopped dead still so suddenly that Brynlee rammed into him.

"What?" she asked, annoyed.

Eli gazed in front of him and walked around the stand, mesmerized. The gold brick. It was there, just there, in the center of the room.

"It's that small? I thought it would be bigger," Bryce said. Everyone stared at him, and he put his hands up defensively. "I'm not saying - I'm just saying."

The gold reflected the bright fluorescent lights. It was about a foot long and half a foot tall. It sat there, with no guards. The others made a semicircle around it. Brynlee and Mia walked into the room as the others stood petrified with awe. They were enchanted by the gold that was sitting in plain sight. No one knew what to do. Bryce was the only one who broke the semicircle. He had stopped in his tracks slightly to the left of the doorway, staring with his mouth wide open.

"Well, what are we waiting for?" Bryce rushed forward to grab it, but Eli's voice stopped him.

"No, wait!"

Bryce looked at him like he was stupid. "But—"

"No, if just one of us grabs it...then..." He turned to Brynlee, who was trying to hide her angry tears, and at Joseph, who seemed to be having more visions he could not escape.

The sound of fighting drifted into the stunned room.

"Then what?" Travis asked tightly.

"Then only our team will get to go free. League Two will get whatever the punishment is. We can't let that happen because we would never have gotten here without them."

Brynlee's grateful look made him uneasy.

"Who takes it, then?" Travis asked, rocking back and forth with nervous energy.

"You pick, Eli," Harper said. He looked at her, stunned.

"You are our leader, Eli; you should do it," Mia said.

"No," he said.

"No?" Bryce asked. "Are we not going to take it?"

"No." Eli looked around the group. "I am not the one who used up my whole life trying to win our freedom."

"But—" Harper started.

"I don't remember it. I don't remember Harper, Travis, Bryce, and everyone else. You all remember, well, maybe not Silvia. But for the majority of us, you all have been through so much more."

"Pick already!" Bryce complained.

"I think - I think that Silvia and Mia should do it."

They both looked startled.

"But I didn't—" Silvia started to refuse, but Mia stepped forward.

"We do it together, Silvia."

Silvia met her eyes and nodded. She hugged Travis one last time, then Mia and Silvia made eye contact.

They each approached the brick from the opposite side. They raised their hands reverently to pick it up when a gunshot split the silence.

The excitement that had been on Bryce's face turned into one of fright and pain. His eyes rolled up in his head, and he fell on his face. Everyone gaped in disbelief at Bryce's motionless body. Then, people from League One emerged from the door, each with someone from Leagues Four and Two. They all had a gun at their head or a knife at their throat. The captives struggled. They entered the room and surrounded Eli's team.

A man in a wheelchair, missing one arm, rolled into the room. "Did you really think that it would be that easy?"

Chapter 16

Eli berated himself for his stupidity. Mia was right; he was a stupid idiot. If he had not kept them talking, then they could have gotten the brick sooner and out of there faster. Now, look at where he had gotten them. He should have listened to Bryce.

Bryce! His heart yearned to hear one of his sarcastic comments. But Bryce's body was still. Harper shook with silent sobs as she stared at her friend's motionless body.

Eli looked at Mia with pleading eyes. He did not want to say anything wrong. Mia shifted and put her hands down.

"Good girl," the man purred.

Eli's hands curled into fists. *Girl? That's what he dares call Mia?*

"We aren't giving up," she said, staring at the man.

Eli's eyes drifted over the people who were in the grips of League One. Some he recognized, some he did not. A young boy who could not have been younger than nine was being threatened with a knife. The woman next to him was Eli's mom. Eli stepped back in shock.

"Mom," he whispered.

Her brown hair swung in her face as she struggled with her captor. Mia's eyes flitted around the circle as she calculated who was in greater danger. Eli shot Kayla a look that she clearly understood. She concentrated on the man in the wheelchair, but nothing happened. Eli blinked in surprise. No drowsy sensation slugged his brain. The man in the chair gave Kayla a look, an amused smile playing on his face.

"That won't work here. You walked into our trap."

She looked at him, startled.

"None of your so-called powers will work here," he said.

Mia tried to run and, Eli assumed, punch the man in the face, but her steps were in slow-motion, even for a normal person. Kayla slumped to the floor, yawning and trying to stay awake.

"It only counters onto yourselves," the man drawled. The man was right. Eli tried to fly, but he felt as heavy as a brick. Harper looked too scared to try her blessing.

"Ah, but it obviously does not work for these two." He wheeled over to where Brynlee had collapsed on the floor next to her brother. She clutched her head. Joseph's eyes were closed tightly. He waved his hands in front of him as if he were in mid-battle.

"Such a pity," the man said, clearly not meaning it. Eli's gaze followed the man's progress around the room. "You know if you really wanted to win, you would not have talked for so long."

Eli felt a roaring in his stomach.

"I know, such a brave soul. This one will be worth it." The man circled Mia, who stiffened. He grabbed one of her hands and examined it. "Yes," he said as if appraising a piece of food he was about to eat.

"Get your hands off her," Eli raged, stepping forward.

The man looked at him in surprise. "Eli, a pleasure to meet you and your girlfriend."

"She's not my girlfriend," Eli retorted in Mia's honor. She looked at him gratefully.

"Ah, pity. She's a good-looking one."

Mia tensed. "What do you want?" she snapped.

"I want you both to back off from the brick and surrender. Leave."

"Ha!" Harper had found the guts to speak.

The man approached her, and she looked sorry that she had uttered anything. She shrank back, tear streaks staining her face.

"And you must be Harper."

She turned green. "How—"

"Oh, I know all of you quite well. I have been watching you for a while now." He continued to roll around the room regally.

"S—" Eli started.

The man interrupted, "H. S. *M!* So stupid, we all know your real names here. You need not use silly code. Now, missies, step back, or else."

The League One fighter holding the boy jerked his dagger up above the boy's panicked face.

"What are you going to do?" Travis asked, sounding scared.

The man in the wheelchair said, "Oh, just threaten some people if you don't cooperate. It's your choice."

Eli swallowed hard. "Let them go," Eli commanded.

"No. Just back off from the B. R. I. C. K."

Everyone looked at him blankly. "Back off the what?" Mia asked.

"Brick! Don't you people know how to spell?" the man asked in exasperation.

"Uhh…" Travis was paralyzed.

"Chance, one done," the man in the wheelchair drawled.

Eli turned as movement in his peripheral vision caught his attention. No one had time to do anything.

The man holding the boy raised his dagger and rammed it right through the boy's head. A big, scary *something* filled Eli's stomach. The boy yelled and went limp. The dagger stuck out the other side of the boy's skull with blood dripping from it.

"No!"

The anguished cry made Eli turn to see a woman fighting furiously against her captor's grip.

"Lance! No!"

The woman's crying made Eli want to do something to help her, but he could not.

"How could you?" Eli rounded on the man and stormed forward—but halted as the man aimed a gun at Mia's head.

"Careful, you don't want your girlfriend's head blown off, now do you?"

Eli's fists clenched. Mia did her best to act as if no gun existed, aiming death at her. He admired her even more for that. They were in an impossible situation because of him.

Because of him, a young boy had died. Because of him…

"Yes," the man said, staring at Eli. "I know what you are thinking."

Is he putting these thoughts in my head? he thought angrily.

The man's face twisted. "You know? How?" Understanding dawned on his face. "Ah, you are a smart one."

Brynlee blinked her eyes open and sat up groggily. "What's going on? Did we win? What?" She shook her head to clear it, trying not to feel all the fear in the room. "E—what?"

"They have us," he told her.

"Eli! No! Take the brick! Don't listen to them!" MaKenzee's shout came from behind Eli. He turned to see his mom struggling against her captor.

"Mom, I can't let so many people die."

"My life doesn't matter to me as much as you do! Tell Mia and Silvia to take it!"

Her captor pressed the blade against her throat. "Shut up," the guard snarled. His mom's eyes told him what she wanted him to do. His eyes stung with tears.

"Decide," the man in the wheelchair egged him. He continued aiming the gun at Mia's head.

Eli made eye contact with Mia. He could not let her die. No way - he could not live with himself if he knew that he was the reason. And yet... He glanced at his mom, who continued to struggle uselessly.

Another person with a dagger came behind his mom. The two readied their daggers so that if she tried to run forward, she would impale herself. Eli started sweating.

"Get the brick," his mom repeated.

The boy's mom continued sobbing as she gazed with tear-streaked eyes at her nine-year-old's body, limp in his captor's arms. Eli's gaze went to Bryce's motionless body on the ground, then to his friends' faces. Travis, scared and concerned. Silvia, who stood, frozen. Mia, a firm look on her face. Kayla, rubbing her eyes to try and stay awake. Harper, who had tears in her eyes as she looked at the scene, shaking and helpless to do anything. Brynlee, who had a hand clenched around her dagger but was unwilling to do anything that might jeopardize their team. Joseph, who lay on the floor, curled into a ball.

Joseph yelled, his eyes flying open and revealing unexplainable horror. "No!"

Gideon's roar could be heard from many hallways away. "Norah!"

Eli and his team started in shock.

"No, no! G, move! Get out of there!" Joseph cried. He got to his knees and tried to shake away the image. "No!"

"Joseph!" Brynlee reached for her brother.

The man in the chair moved his gun on Brynlee.

"Brynlee!" Eli figured that if League One had a machine that somehow knew all their names, it wouldn't hurt to call everyone by their name here.

A split second later, chaos erupted all around them.

His mom's voice rang out at the same time that Sheldon appeared in the doorway and somehow blew fire as if a bomb had just gone off in his mouth. A handful of League One's allies were startled and shied away from the blistering heat and anger coming from Sheldon.

MaKenzee's voice rang out. "Mia, do it for me!"

Eli spun around to stare at his mom right as both her captors flung their daggers forward, MaKenzee lunging towards her son. Her eyes bulged as the daggers split through her skin at full force. Blood poured from her sides. Her body slumped over the daggers as the two guards dropped them and stepped towards Eli.

Anger boiled over in Eli. He stepped forward to meet the two guards, but a rough hand grabbed the back of his shirt and pulled him away. He looked back to see Gideon's horrified face as he saw their mom's dead body, oozing blood onto the floor. A clatter from the middle of the room made Eli turn as Gideon transformed into his other form and bounded towards the two guards who had killed his mom.

"What! *No!*" the man in the chair roared in rage. "How!" He aimed his fist at something black that protruded from the corner of the ceiling. "You imbeciles got distracted!" The man was insane.

The world seemed to go in slow motion. Fire billowed from behind Silvia and Mia. The man in the wheelchair skirted around the flames that were trying to devour him, yelling nonsense about the defense mechanism being down, about stupid electronics that didn't work.

Mia and Silvia's hands landed on the gold bar just as Joseph made it to his feet, leaning against his sister. The two girls' hands lifted the bar, and a loud shriek filled the air. The lights flashed. Eli had to focus hard to keep from blacking out.

"What now? I thought it would be done when we had it!" Travis bellowed.

Eli got a sudden idea. "Follow me!"

Battle flew around them. Flashes of light, screams, random weapons flew in every direction.

Harper understood what Eli meant. "Surround them!" she ordered.

Travis ended up with his back to Silvia. Harper put her back to Mia. Brynlee managed to drag her brother over to the group as Silvia and Mia made their way through the fights. Sheldon was busy keeping the enemy at bay with his flames. Gideon's brawling made Eli feel empty inside; he felt fear but did his best to hide it. He wove his way between fighters who were screaming and shouting. He tripped over a body but did not have time to see who it was.

"Eli! We can't keep up!" Harper gasped, stumbling along. Eli's friends, who were trying to protect the brick, were having trouble walking backwards. Someone from League Four spotted them and started to celebrate. Eli's look made them halt, understanding his intentions. He didn't want to draw attention to his group.

A brilliant idea popped into his head.

"Fall behind me!" he roared to the group of fighting arms

and limbs. The few people who heard and understood swarmed around Mia and Silvia, making a tighter circle around the brick.

The group burst out of League One's base. Silvia's face tightened with effort to keep the brick in her grasp.

They continued walking as fast as they could in their awkward huddle. The new alarm startled several of their team's backup so that they stumbled out of formation.

Mia screamed, and the group halted altogether. Eli rushed to find Mia on the ground, clutching her leg.

"Go!" Mia cried. The bar slipped in Silvia's hands.

"Kayla! Grab the brick!" Eli yelled.

Kayla stepped into Mia's spot.

"Harper, to the hole!" Eli bellowed.

"But—"

"Go! I'll be there when I can!" Eli kneeled by Mia as several people from League Four surrounded the two to protect them.

"Go with them," Mia said.

"I can't leave you."

"Yes, you can." She clutched her leg. It was bent at a strange angle.

"Don't be an idiot," Eli snapped.

She managed a weak smile. "Go with the others. I'll

manage."

"No," Eli stubbornly refused. He put one of her arms over his shoulder and helped her stand up. They took one hesitant step forward, and Mia started to fall. She grabbed Eli's arm to stop herself from hitting the pavement. Her face twisted, and she gritted her teeth as she tried to straighten herself up. They tried again.

Fighting swarmed around them. If it weren't for the people who had stepped forward to protect them, they definitely would have been slaughtered. Mia tried again and nearly fell.

"Teleport us." Mia gasped.

"I don't remember how-" Eli's mind blurred. "Take my hand." Eli offered his free hand to her.

"No," she panted.

"It's the only way you will make it to where we need to go," he insisted.

"Idiot." She took his hand and gripped it hard.

They managed to hobble, with her leaning almost all her weight on Eli. They thumped and stumbled down sidewalks, following the sound of battle. They finally caught up with their friends, who appeared unopposed, having defeated their enemies at hand. They split apart to show Kayla and Silvia still holding the brick next to the wall. Eli lowered Mia to the ground. She took her hand back faster than one would have thought comfortable with a broken leg.

"What's wrong?" he asked.

"What do we do now? We'll be cornered soon," Kayla said.

"My arms are killing me," Silvia confessed.

"Through the hole," Eli said.

"The what?" Kayla asked.

"Look!" Harper pointed to the bottom of the wall. The two holding the brick bent down to peer through the hole.

"What?" Kayla repeated.

"It's just big enough for you to crawl through," Eli said.

"But what happens after that?" Silvia asked.

"I don't know," Eli admitted. "But we need to try. An army can't easily get through there all at once."

"But we don't know anything about that place." Silvia's hands slipped on the brick.

"Siv." Travis stepped forward and put a hand on her shoulder. "You can do this." He kissed her cheek. "We will be right behind you."

Silvia nodded solemnly.

"Let's do this," Kayla said, setting her jaw but looking terrified at the same time.

The people who had helped keep the brick safe formed a

semicircle around Mia, Eli, Silvia, and Kayla as Silvia and Kayla crouched. Silvia started shaking as she looked through the hole.

"How will we fit?" she asked.

"You will have to slide through," Eli said, bending down once more to look at the amazing sight of the green things and the other mysterious objects on the other side of their prison, for that was indeed what it felt like.

Suddenly, fighting broke out from the edge of the semicircle. People from Base One had caught up to them, and *oh no* -

League Three was here.

"Eli, hurry!" Travis ordered.

"Go! Kayla, you first."

She looked at Eli with horror on her face. "But—"

"It'll be okay." *I hope.* "I'll be through as soon as I can!"

Kayla got down on her belly with Silvia and started inching her way backwards through the hole. She paused for a moment, frightened when her feet made it through.

"What?"

"The ground is soft! What if I fall through?"

"I hope you won't," Eli said, thinking about the strange thing dancing in the green.

Kayla pushed herself through the hole and paused, her

hands just barely inside the base, clutching the gold brick.

"It's bizarre!" Kayla called through the hole as Silvia made it inside.

Someone smacked into Eli.

"Eli!"

Mia's scream jolted him. He turned. It was — oh no, the person who had tried to kill him and Mia when he had first woken up. The man unleashed dagger-like fingernails as he approached Eli. Eli backed up as he clumsily groped for his sword. He tripped over Silvia's legs and fell backwards. His head smacked against the brick wall, and his vision glazed over for a moment.

The man loomed over him when a shrill noise sounded from all directions. Everyone froze and looked around. Eli jumped back in surprise, landing against Mia, who yelped in pain. All action halted.

The wall disintegrated like water cascading to the ground.

Kayla sat on the green stuff as if mesmerized. She ran her hands through it in wonder. Silvia stood up and looked behind her to see stunned armies staring towards her. The brick lay forgotten on the ground.

They could see so many new sights. The brown things that went up from the green things ended in more green that moved slightly. Something was pushing against Eli, and apparently everyone. The group jumped, and some started panicking. Above them, blue stretched in an endless arc, and there were white puffy shapes up there and one blindingly bright yellow ball that shot daggers into the blue. Further down, on the cement, were more buildings. The colorful, thicker, green things were everywhere, lining the pathway.

"What?" Eli asked. Eli's eyes drank in the scene as he walked forward and studied the line separating the concrete from the green. By now, Kayla was lying full out in the green stuff and luxuriating in its soft touch. Weapons were dropped as the expanse of green drew people.

"Eli…" Mia's whisper jolted him back. He stumbled over to where Mia was and helped her up. He walked her over to the edge. "What? Where is this?" she asked.

It seemed as if the people in the once-fortress had forgotten all about their rivalry, forgetting their anger. The bright thing in the sky shone so brightly.

"Where is this?" Mia whispered.

"I don't know."

Kayla laughed, drawing their attention to her. She was rolling over and over in the green that was bending at her weight. She stopped and jumped to her feet. "What are you all waiting fo—"

She was cut off as a cool voice from somewhere said, "Well, well. You did it. After so many decades."

Chapter 17

Eli looked around. His eyes adjusted to the new surroundings, and saw a woman in the shadow between two buildings. She emerged into the light. She stood tall and regal, with blond hair and stern blue eyes. Two men stood behind her like bodyguards. Eli would have stepped forward but was too afraid of the green things.

"It's okay. You guinea pigs can come onto the grass," she said. *Guinea pigs?* Eli thought. *What or who are those?*

Mia, with Eli's help, tentatively stepped onto the—as the woman called it—*grass*.

Everyone else stood back. The ground squished slightly. He shifted uneasily as Mia clutched him—despite her annoyance—harder.

"What?" she asked, looking down.

"Who are you? Where is this place?" Eli asked.

The woman laughed a tinkling laugh. "Ah, I should have known. This is the world." She spread her arms out wide. "You have been in an enclosed space for centuries, oh," - she gave a high-pitched giggle - "decades."

Everyone stared at her. Silence spread as the stunned

warriors took in the newcommer.

"I'm Iva," the woman said as she dropped her arms. She wore a white dress that draped down to cover her feet. She stepped onto the green. Oh, the grass. The strange feeling came again, and the green on the brown rippled. The assembly jumped and started cowering, trying to duck under it. The woman's dress moved with the green.

"It's okay," she soothed. "It's the wind or the breeze. It's both."

People stood up again, looking nervous.

"What do you want?" Eli managed to ask.

Just then, more people turned up and halted in stunned amazement. Gideon, limping, managed to force his way to the edge of the pavement.

"What's going on? What happened?"

Eli turned, slowly as he was still supporting Mia, to face his brother.

"We won," he said.

Gideon stepped back. "What?"

"The brick. Look, Kayla and Silvia got it out," Eli said.

Kayla was watching everything with wonder. Silvia looked up at the blueness above, her dark hair cascading down and waving in the…breeze. Wind. Whatever it was.

"Welcome." Iva's voice was soft, almost too soft. Eli looked towards her as she walked forward. "Come. Everyone, from League Four and Two."

"And why should we trust you?" The man who had attacked Eli stepped out of the crowd, his nails still unleashed.

Iva's gaze snapped to him. "Why shouldn't you?"

"You are responsible for our enclosure." He turned to face the assembly. "She's the one we blame!" People started, realizing what he was saying. No flicker of fear flashed through Iva's regal face. "Now, we shall revenge our ancestors!" He moved towards her, and another person raised a gun and pointed it at Iva's forehead.

"Stop." Her voice echoed through the wall-less space. The men stopped. Mia shifted in Eli's support.

"Let me at her," Mia hissed into Eli's ear, as the assembly was dead silent, even the man who had talked back to Iva. Eli hardly registered what Mia said, mesmerized by Iva.

"I am the one giving you freedom, aren't I?" Her expression showed confidence. She knew who was really in charge: her. Nothing else mattered. "Right." People blinked and looked around, somewhat confused. "Now, Leagues Four and Two!"

People stepped forward, careful with approaching a woman who seemed to emanate such power, even more power and confidence than Mia. Eli's hands grew clammy. He took a step forward, before indicating to Mia that he was going to obey the woman. Mia yelped as she was jerked forward.

"Mia, sorry!" Eli helped her to a more stable position.

Iva's cold eyes snapped to the two. "You are wounded?" Iva asked.

Eli looked at Mia, who refused to make eye contact with him. She looked at Iva instead. Mia's hair rippled in the breeze and shone even brighter. Eli's heart fluttered for the millionth time.

"Yes," Eli said.

"We will take care of them. Leaders, follow me. The rest of you, stay here. We'll be back."

"I'm not leaving you," Eli said quietly to Mia as some medics came out of a building.

"Yes, you are," Mia retorted. "I'll be fine."

"But—"

"Don't be an idiot."

"Ahem." Eli looked around.

Brynlee raised her eyebrows at Eli. She was pretty scuffed up as well. She had cuts on her face, and her hair wasn't at its best. "Let's go," she said. Eli had forgotten that she was the leader of her small group.

Several leaders emerged from the crowd and stepped onto the grass. Most looked frightened. Some younger children slipped their feet out of their shoes and felt the grass with their bare toes. Their faces broke into smiles. Once all the leaders from Leagues Four and Two were standing in the grass, Mia spoke.

"Put me down. Go with them," she said.

"I can't," Eli said.

"Yes, you can, dummy."

He lowered her. The medics from the other building helped her up again. He watched as the medics helped her into the building along with the other wounded people.

"Brother." Eli jumped. He turned to see Gideon standing in the grass, looking nervous. "You did it."

"I did not—"

"Come, we have no time to waste," Iva cut him off. Iva turned and started walking down the sidewalk. Eli looked back at Harper. Her eyes flitted to him, and they nodded together. They had a silent communication: *see you in a bit.*

The group of leaders, about forty in all, followed slowly, freaking out about the shadows that were cast on the ground by the green and brown things. Iva just giggled and said that it was okay to walk through them. They made it to a quiet road and walked along it for a while until they entered a red brick building. It had one large room with a doorway at the other end. The group gathered in a long arc around Iva.

She turned to them and smiled, but it was a sour smile.

"Well, you did it. You worked together to win your prize, and here it is." Everyone leaned in closer as she pulled out...a yellow, flat thing. She had a pile of them in her hands.

"Just show the cashier this card, and they will let you go. We will cover the cost for you. It's unlimited." She started passing the yellow cards that read *Please swipe card,* along with a series of numbers. She gave each leader a precise amount of cards. She somehow knew how many people were in each person's group. Eli found that odd.

"Now enjoy yourselves! Go! Explore the world beyond and enjoy it while you can!"

The group started to disperse. Eli stood there, staring at Iva. Gideon touched his shoulder, startling Eli. "Let's go, brother."

"How did you know how many people were in my team? How did you know not to give any for Addy and Layla?" Eli asked, ignoring Gideon.

Iva smiled winningly at him. "No matter."

"And what did you mean, *while you can*?"

"So many questions, Mr. Johnson," she said. Eli started at the sound of his last name. "The world awaits you, and Miss Mia awaits."

Gideon tugged Eli out of the room and into the brightness. The two walked down the road, back to the place where they had left their friends.

"I don't believe it. You did it, brother," Gideon said.

"You are different," Eli told him.

"What?"

"Not as, umm…fierce." He flinched, remembering what had happened when he had called Mia fierce.

"There is no pressure on me anymore. I don't know… I'd better go find Norah; she was wounded pretty bad."

They reached the place where people were carefully stepping onto the grass. A few children ran and played tag, laughing and rolling in it as Kayla had. League Three was nowhere in sight, weapons still scattered on the ground, completely forgotten. Eli's eyes roamed the area and spotted Harper. He walked over the grass to her. She was standing on the concrete where he had left her, drinking in the new sights.

"Why don't you try this, umm…grass? Have you seen Mia?" Eli asked.

"No, I haven't."

"I hope she's okay."

"She'll be okay." Harper put her hand on his shoulder. "You'll see. You'll get her."

Tears sprang to his eyes.

"What?"

"My mom said something like that." He sniffled and tried to hide his tears from the other people surrounding him.

"I'm sorry, Eli." She wrapped her arms around him, not unlike the hug his mom had given him. He stayed there for a while, grateful for one of his closest friends.

"So." He stepped into the grass. "Ready to try it out?"

Harper's eyes shone with happy tears. "I don't know." She looked at it. "I wanted to feel this from the time that we saw it. But now I'm frightened."

"It's okay," he said.

She slipped her shoes off and slowly set one foot on the green grass. She looked up at him, and a broad smile spread across her face. She slowly put her other foot into it. She had her arms stretched out as if the ground were uneven and she might lose her balance. Eli reached out to help her feel steady. She took his hand.

"It's okay," Eli encouraged. *I think...*

She moved her toes and grinned. "If only Bryce—"

She cut herself off and looked away, taking deep breaths. Eli suddenly felt a great sadness that Bryce, his mom, and that young boy were not experiencing this with them.

Bryce... Gone.

Harper seemed to have gained enough confidence to drop Eli's hand. They were quiet for some time as silent tears slipped down Harper's face. Eli had known that Harper and Bryce had a close friendship. *And what had that thing I had walked in on been about? It seemed to be about something more than Harper having a breakdown.*

Eli remembered the yellow cards. He gave one to Harper and told her about it. He hunted down the rest of the people from their team, other than Mia, who had not returned from the ward. He ventured over to where Brynlee and Joseph were sitting cross-legged on the grass. Joseph had his hands to his eyes.

"What's up?" Eli asked.

"Stupid visions!" *Is Joseph crying?* It sounded like it.

"Hey, man, it's okay. We won."

"They did not. There are generations of families." He lowered his hands to reveal red eyes. "It's horrible what's happening to them... But it's not like my normal visions. It's all blurry."

"Wait—" Eli had an insane thought. "You can't, can you?"

"Can't what?" Brynlee asked.

"Can you see the future?"

Joseph blinked at him. "I don't know. Some visions are blurry, like that one with Mia."

"Mia? What one with Mia?" Eli asked.

Brynlee gritted her teeth. "Stop that."

"What?" Eli asked.

She rolled her eyes. "The heart-fluttering emotion. The feeling you get when you picture her. All that annoying stuff."

Eli stared at her. "Who?"

"Idiot!" He knew who she was talking about. "Mia." As if she had summoned her, Mia stepped out of the building that she had been in.

"Oh, for Pete's sake!" Brynlee grumbled. Brynlee turned her back on Eli.

Mia had her leg in a cast and was leaning on crutches. Eli stood up from where he had sat down on the grass. She hobbled across the pavement to look at the green.

Harper ran over to her and hugged her. "You're okay!"

"Of course I am," he heard Mia say.

"Just go," Brynlee said.

Eli walked towards Mia like a zombie. Harper turned at his approach and stepped back. Mia watched him with no expression. He opened his mouth, but nothing came out.

"I—uh…" He stepped closer and opened his arms for a hug.

Mia looked at him and raised her eyebrows. "Hi."

He dropped his arms and scratched his arm. "So, you're

okay." He looked around, then back to her.

"Obviously," she said.

Harper looked like she wished that she could sink into the ground. "So…Mia, have you tried this grass stuff yet?"

Mia started at Harper's question. She and Eli had been staring at each other, both in different ways.

"I have been on it before…" Mia answered. "But I wasn't really paying attention. What do you think it feels like?"

Harper said, "Soothing. Sometimes there is something sharp, but it doesn't hurt that much."

Mia clumsily set her crutches on the grass. Eli held out his hand in an offer to help, but Mia death-glared him to stop.

"I've tried it already."

He stepped back. She thumped her cast on the grass and paused.

"It's firm, I promise," Harper said.

Mia put her other foot down and looked around. "Is this it? This is the outside world? Smaller than I thought."

"You sound like Bryce," Eli said.

Harper's eyes filled with tears, her shoulders shaking.

"I'm sorry, Harper. I didn't mean to make you upset." He swallowed the lump in his throat as Harper shook her head.

"He could have been here with us," she sobbed, burying her face in her hands. She wiped her eyes and looked up. The sudden flow of tears had faded. They had all learned to be tough and not show emotion in the league.

"What now?" she asked, trying to act like nothing had happened even though Eli could still see the glimmer of tears in her eyes.

"I don't know." He looked around uselessly. He spotted Travis across the grass. Silvia was hugging her mom, but her dad did not seem to be present. Eli's heart sank. He walked over to them. Mia and Harper followed.

"What's up?" he asked Travis.

Travis watched his girlfriend with sad eyes. "Her dad didn't make it out…"

"I'm so sorry, Silvia," Eli said. She looked at him with a tear trickling down her face.

Her mom stepped forward. "I must thank you for saving my daughter."

"No biggie, it was mostly Addy—" Eli cut himself off, thinking of his lost - friend?

"We should find where we are going to live," Silvia's mom told her.

"Um…how do we do that?"

~

Hours later, Eli found himself walking along a sidewalk. Strange people were walking past him - many, many strange people. Harper walked next to him, and beside her, Mia thumped and bumped along. Travis walked on Eli's other side, and Kayla skipped on ahead. She stopped and turned to them.

"Look! This is amazing!" She pointed to a coffee shop that stood on their side of the sidewalk. "It's a coffee shop! It's a miracle! Places actually *sell* coffee!" She clattered into it.

The group paused, occasionally chatting while they waited for Kayla. She had already downed a large-sized coffee and about half a dozen other caffeinated drinks.

"Hey, guys!"

Eli turned to face Brynlee and Joseph. Joseph looked a lot more stable than he had a few hours ago.

"What's up?" Eli asked.

"Nothing much. Trying to figure out where to stay. For some reason, some of the shop owners won't let us live in the buildings."

"We should do that too; it will be dark soon," Travis said.

Kayla ran out of the shop with a big fufu drink in her hands. She bounced on the balls of her feet, grinning. "This place is amazing!"

"Roof!"

"Hey, did you hear that?" he asked. They all paused.

"Roof! Roof!"

"It's the thing!" Harper shouted, following the familiar sound.

"Harper, what?" Brynlee asked as she hurried to keep up. The *roofs!* got louder as they ran down the sidewalk.

Mia could still move impressively fast, even with crutches. "I need to find Norah," Mia grumbled.

They turned a corner to see a long stretch of grass with the brown things here and there. A girl stood under one of the green parts and threw a ball. The thing ran and caught it in its mouth. They stepped onto the grass. It noticed them and dropped the ball. It bounded over to them, shaking its rear in delight.

"Roof!" It slobbered all over Eli's hand. Everyone but Harper and Eli stepped back, frightened.

"Thing!" Harper bent down to scratch its neck.

"What did you call him?" the strange girl asked as she walked up to them. "Thing, why? Why would you call him that?"

"Uhh…what is it?"

The girl stared at Harper like she was the most naive person she had ever met.

"He's a dog." She said it like it should be obvious.

"Dog," Harper said, trying out the new word.

"His name is Emmitt."

"Emmitt. I like that!" Eli said, bending down to pet Emmitt, who had bounced over to him when he had said his name.

"You aren't from around here, are you? No offense, just how could you not know what a dog is?"

"Oh…um…" Harper looked at Mia.

"Kinda hard to explain," Mia said.

Travis bent down and held out his hand. Emmitt trotted over to Travis and sniffed his hand. "Strange, it's like a tiny Gideon!"

"Gideon? Is that one of your pets?"

"Pets? What is that?"

The girl gaped in shock.

~

Three weeks later, Eli, Harper, Joseph, and Mia were strolling down a sidewalk on a sunny afternoon. Mia had seen Norah and gotten her leg healed and was perfectly happy to walk without help.

"Things can change in the blink of an eye. I feel like we just met," Joseph commented.

"They sure do," Eli agreed.

"And I'm glad we get along," Harper said.

"Me too," Joseph agreed. "I don't know what Brynlee and I would have done if we didn't bunk with you guys." Eli, Travis, and Joseph had found a house to rent, much to the raised eyebrows of the landowner. Harper, Kayla, Brynlee, and Mia had a house together as well.

"This place always has something new to show us," Harper said.

Mia stopped and bent down to tie her shoe. Eli stopped to wait for her. "Go on, I'll catch up."

Eli turned and continued walking down the sidewalk. He felt as if he could fly without even trying.

Sad memories of Bryce and his mom came to him from time to time, though fewer of his mom than Bryce. Harper still cried over Bryce now and then, but he couldn't blame her. She had known Bryce her whole life, and with him being snatched out of her life so suddenly must be devastating. Eli thought about Mia. He thought of some of his last conversations with his mom. *You'll get her someday.* He looked up at the blue sky; he was learning more new words every day and was ready to learn more about the outside world. The breeze-wind blew against his face. He closed his eyes, taking a deep breath, relishing the calm afternoon. He opened his eyes again and smiled as he looked over at Joseph.

Joseph blinked hard.

"You okay, dude?" Eli asked.

"Um." Joseph paused. "I think… I…" He stopped and clutched his head.

"More visions?" Travis asked.

"Yeah. Weird ones, fuzzy." He shook his head as if to clear it again.

Mia's voice floated to Eli's ears, and his brain immediately awoke, becoming alert as his insides searched for her attention. Mia was laughing.

"Brynlee!" Mia chided.

Eli smiled. Every time Brynlee came to hang out with them, she would creep up behind Mia and put her dagger to her throat. Though, she had learned not to do that in public anymore as it caused too much commotion, and someone would call the security people with more Emmitts. He expected to hear her running to catch up with the group. He looked at Joseph again, whose face had paled.

Then, he heard Mia's scream.

Eli's face went slack. He whipped around. Mia never screamed like that. His eyes were fixed on the spot where she had been a moment ago. No Mia. No Brynlee. His heart pumped blood into his ears, his head filling with a strange sensation.

"What happened?" Joseph was next to him.

"I - I don't know!" Eli gasped, starting to run for the spot where Mia had just been.

The sound of squealing car tires echoed. An engine roared. He turned towards the gap between the two buildings and was face to face with a black car screaming its way towards him.

Eli's instincts shot him into the air, and, as he looked down, he saw Mia, her hands pressed against the back window of the car, a frantic expression that he had never seen on her face, pounding on the glass.

"Mia!" he bellowed and shot to the ground, landing painfully, his brain overwrought with worry.

Joseph ran up to him. "Man, what?"

"We need to go after her, now." He started running, but Joseph stopped him.

"We need a plan; we don't know who they are."

"They have *her!*" Eli roared, stepping closer to Joseph, fists tightening. "That's all - we are letting them get away!"

"Hang on, Mia's been taken?" Harper asked, worry spreading across her face.

"Yes!" Eli said impatiently, stomping his foot like a raging child. "And we need to go save her."

"But I thought - I thought this world was different," Harper stumbled out.

"We *all* did, Harper," Eli snapped. Harper's face crumpled.

"Sorry, but Mia's in danger."

"Then what are we waiting for?" Harper asked.

Eli threw his hands up in exasperation. "Exactly my question!"

"C'mon then!" Harper started running.

"Harper, shouldn't we have a plan?" Joseph called after her, but Eli and Harper were already many paces ahead.

Eli's head spun, in more ways than one. Eli was so busy thinking that he forgot to concentrate on where he was going, and he tripped over something, something that went, *"Roof!"*

The End